THE GREEK

They're the men who ~~have everything~~
except brides…

Wealth, power, charm—what else could a
heart-stoppingly handsome tycoon need?
In THE GREEK TYCOONS mini-series
you have already been introduced to some
gorgeous Greek multimillionaires
who are in need of wives.

Now it's the turn of favourite
Modern™ author Melanie Milburne,
with her attention-grabbing romance

The Greek's Convenient Wife

This tycoon has met his match,
and he's decided he *has* to have her…
whatever that takes!

Melanie Milburne says: 'I am married to a surgeon, Steve, and have two gorgeous sons, Paul and Phil. I live in Hobart, Tasmania, where I enjoy an active life as a long-distance runner and nationally ranked top ten Master's swimmer. I also have a Master's Degree in Education, but my children totally turned me off the idea of teaching! When not running or swimming, I write, and when I'm not doing all of the above I'm reading. And if someone could invent a way for me to read during a four-kilometre swim I'd be even happier!'

Recent titles by the same author:

HIS INCONVENIENT WIFE
THE BLACKMAIL PREGNANCY
THE AUSTRALIAN'S MARRIAGE DEMAND
THE ITALIAN'S MISTRESS

THE GREEK'S CONVENIENT WIFE

BY
MELANIE MILBURNE

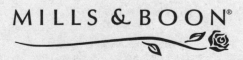

MILLS & BOON®

To Bruce and Nadine
You are such fun to be around, and have brought
immeasurable joy to our lives. This one is for both of you,
and when you read it you'll know exactly why!

*First published in Great Britain 2005
Harlequin Mills & Boon Limited,
Eton House, 18-24 Paradise Road, Richmond, Surrey TW9 1SR*

© Melanie Milburne 2005

ISBN 0 263 84140 5

*Set in Times Roman 10 on 11 pt.
01-0405-57505*

*Printed and bound in Spain
by Litografía Rosés, S.A., Barcelona*

CHAPTER ONE

MADDISON stared at her younger brother in abject horror.

'What do you mean you sank his yacht?'

A petulant scowl took up residence on Kyle Jones's nine-teen-year-old face.

'He deserved it.'

'Oh, my God.' She put her head in her hands as she struggled to gain control of her sky-rocketing emotions.

'I thought you'd be happy,' Kyle said with a hint of pique. 'After all, he's the one who ruined Dad. I thought you'd be pleased I made a stand at long last.'

'Kyle.' She lifted her tortured gaze to his. 'Do you have any idea of what you've done?'

He set his shoulders defiantly. 'I don't care. He had it coming to him.'

Maddison shut her eyes. 'I can't believe I'm hearing this.'

'It's all right,' he reassured her. 'He has no idea who did it.'

She opened her eyes to face him. 'How can you possibly know that for sure? People like Demetrius Papasakis always know who their enemies are.' She got to her feet in agitation and paced the room. 'You do realise what this means, don't you?' She turned to face him once more, her expression pale with worry.

Her brother gave a dismissive shrug. 'What are you so worried about? He's never going to know it was me.'

'Of course he'll know it was you! You've already got a police record! It's not going to take him long to put two and two together and come up with your name, and once he does you can be certain of one thing—he'll make sure you end up in prison.'

'I'm not going to prison,' he said emphatically.

'No, you're not. At least not if I can help it.' She gnawed her bottom lip as she hunted her brain for a solution.

'I'm glad I did it, no matter what you think.' An element of proud defiance had entered Kyle's voice. 'Anyway, it's not as if he can't afford another yacht; he's positively loaded.'

'That's the whole trouble, don't you see?' Desperation was creeping into her tone but there was nothing she could do to stop it. 'Unlike us, he can afford the very best legal advice. You won't have a leg to stand on, especially after that last car you stole.'

'I didn't steal it,' he protested. 'I borrowed it.'

'Don't split hairs, Kyle. You know you stole it and you were incredibly lucky to get out on bail, which I might remind you at this point I have yet to pay back to the bank.'

'I'll pay you back when I get a job,' he promised.

Maddison sighed with frustration. 'And when is that going to be? You've already had three jobs, none of them lasting more than a week. I can't keep covering up for you; at some point you're going to have to take responsibility for your own life. You're nineteen years old, more than old enough to drive and vote. It's about time you stopped blaming everyone else for what's gone wrong in your life and make something good happen instead.'

'Demetrius Papasakis wrecked our lives,' Kyle said bitterly. 'How can you simply sit back and let him get away with it?'

'There are better ways than sinking million dollar boats,' she pointed out wryly. 'We could have gone to him and stated our case, perhaps fought for compensation.'

'Oh yeah, right.' His voice was scathing. 'He'd laugh in our face; he couldn't give a fig for what happened to Dad when he lost his job. And besides, look at the way he treats the latest women in his life; that man doesn't have a conscience.'

Maddison couldn't agree more, but didn't want to encourage her brother's fiery temper. Hardly a day went past without one of the Sydney papers revealing the latest antics of the billionaire playboy, a six-foot-three Greek god of a man with too much money and not enough scruples.

Their father had worked for Demetrius Papasakis as an assistant accountant in the Papasakis hotel chain for years, only to be dismissed without a fair hearing when a question had been raised about the supposed misappropriation of funds. The mud thrown had stuck, and within weeks their father had collapsed with a fatal heart attack, which Maddison knew had been due to the intolerable strain he had faced at the time.

'People like Demetrius Papasakis usually get their comeuppance in the end,' she said instead. 'The trick is to hang around long enough to witness it.'

'Maybe you're right.' The edge of her brother's mouth lifted in a small smile. 'According to yesterday's paper, Papasakis is currently in the middle of yet another relationship scandal, a rich divorcee this time, the ex-wife of one of his business rivals.'

'At the moment I'm not too concerned about the trouble Demetrius Papasakis may or may not be in,' she said. 'The thing I'm concerned with right here and now is how we're going to get you out of the firing line until the dust settles over this boat episode.'

'I'm not afraid of Papasakis,' he said with a lift of his chin.

'I know, more's the pity,' she answered wryly. 'But I am. He'll stop at nothing to pay back a misdemeanour such as this and I don't want to make it too easy for him to do so.'

'What do you think I should do?'

Maddison took a deep breath of resignation before answering. 'You'll have to go into hiding.'

'Run away, you mean?' The look he sent her was brim-full of male affront.

'Not in so many words,' she reassured him. 'I have a friend who is working as a nanny on a cattle property in the Northern Territory. In her last letter she told me of the trouble Gillaroo is having recruiting reliable station hands. I can just about afford to pay for your airfare to get you there. After that the rest is up to you.'

'A station hand?' Kyle wrinkled his nose.

'Listen, Kyle.' She eyeballed him determinedly. 'I'm running out of both money and patience. This is your last chance. If you don't take it I'm going to have to wash my hands and leave you to face the music, but let me warn you the sort of music Papasakis will want to play won't be to your taste.'

'All right,' he said. 'I'll do it, but only because you want me to, not because I'm scared.'

'Believe me, you don't have to be scared,' she said with feeling. 'I'm scared enough for both of us.'

Maddison had not long returned from the airport after her younger brother's departure when the doorbell of her small apartment rang. A flicker of fear brushed the floor of her stomach as she went to answer it, her instincts warning her off opening the door.

The tall, intimidating figure of Demetrius Papasakis stood framed in the doorway, his brown, almost black, eyes glittering as they insolently raked her from head to foot.

Shock rendered her momentarily speechless. How had he known where she lived? And, more to the point, what did he know about her brother's activities the night before?

'Miss Jones, I presume?'

'Th...that's correct.' It annoyed her immensely that her voice had sounded distinctly husky. 'How can I help you?'

'I'd like to speak with your brother.'

Her eyes flickered briefly away from the dark intensity of his.

'He's not here right now.'

'Where is he?' The three words were as sharp as daggers, accusing almost.

'I don't actually know.' She reassured herself that it was the truth; she had no idea what part of the continent Kyle was currently flying over.

'Don't play games with me, Miss Jones,' he warned her silkily. 'I have an issue to discuss with your brother and it would be in his best interests to hear me out.'

'I'm sorry I can't help you.'

She began to close the door in his face but before she could get any weight behind it, he reached out a lean hand and the door slammed back against the wall with a resounding thwack.

She shrank back, her hand going shakily to her throat.

He stepped through the doorway and closed the door behind him with exaggerated care.

'I wouldn't like your neighbours to overhear what I have to say,' he said.

'I'd like you to leave.' She stepped back another step. 'Right now.'

'Before or after I call the police?' He unhooked his mobile phone from the waistband of his trousers.

She swallowed the constriction in her throat as his lean brown fingers began typing in some numbers.

'What's it to be, Miss Jones?' His forefinger paused over the last digit.

Maddison bit her lip.

'I have your brother's probation officer's telephone number right here,' he said. 'Perhaps you'd like to speak to him about your brother's whereabouts last night?'

'He was here, with me,' she said in a thin voice.

He lifted a sceptical brow. 'You expect me to believe that?'

'Believe what you like.'

'You're playing a dangerous game, Miss Jones. Perhaps I'm not making myself clear.' He stepped closer to where she was backed up against the wall. 'I'm not leaving here without information about your brother's whereabouts.'

'I hope you've brought a toothbrush then.' Her sapphire-blue eyes flashed with fire. 'I don't have a spare.'

His eyes glinted with reluctant amusement at her show of spirit.

'Are you offering me your bed?'

'Not a chance,' she returned primly. 'You're not my type.'

He leant one hand on one side of her head and surveyed her up-tilted face in a leisurely manner.

Maddison sucked in a sharp little breath when his fingers captured a strand of her ash-blonde hair, coiling it repeatedly until she was forced to take a tiny step towards him. She could feel the heat of his body this close, his dark eyes so mesmerising she felt as if he was seeing through to her very soul, laying all her innermost secrets bare. She could pick up a faint trace of his citrus-scented aftershave in the air surrounding them, and her bare leg beneath her skirt felt the unmistakable brush of a hard muscled, very male thigh.

'Now, let's try it one more time.' His voice was a silky caress across the sensitised skin of her lips. 'Where is your brother, Miss Jones?'

She sent her tongue out to the tombstone-dryness of her lips. She saw his dark eyes follow the movement and the breath in her chest tightened another notch.

'He's…away,' she croaked.

His brows snapped together in a frown. 'Away?'

She nodded.

'Where?'

'Interstate.'

'Which state?'

'I can't tell you.'

'You will tell me, Miss Jones.' His voice was velvet-covered steel. 'Even if I have to force it out of you.'

'I'm not afraid of you.'

'Are you not?' Amusement gleamed in his eyes. 'Then you should be.'

'Do your worst, Mr Papasakis.' She lifted her chin. 'I'm not easily intimidated.'

'Then I shall have to be very creative and think of an effective tool to bring about your capitulation.' His smile was deliberately sensuous. 'Now won't that be fun?'

She didn't trust herself to reply. Hatred seethed in her belly until she was sure she'd explode with the effort of keeping it under some semblance of control. She knew enough about him to know he wouldn't rest until he exacted some sort of revenge, but as long as she had breath she wasn't going to let him get within a gnat's eyelash of her brother.

'Nothing to say, Miss Jones?' he asked after a tight little silence.

She set her mouth in an intractable line. 'Get out of my apartment.'

'Say please.'

'Go to hell.'

'Now, now, Miss Jones, that's not very hospitable of you, is it?'

'If you don't leave I'll scream.'

'I just love it when a woman screams,' he drawled suggestively.

Maddison's face suffused with outraged colour. 'You're disgusting.'

'And you are aiding and abetting a criminal.'

'My brother is not a criminal,' she ground out through clenched teeth.

'You're living in a fool's paradise, Miss Jones,' he warned her. 'He's already got a record. One more strike and he's out—or should I say inside?'

'I don't know what you're talking about,' she hedged, her cheeks instantly heating.

'Perhaps you will when I tell you I have proof of your brother's lawbreaking tendencies.'

She gave him a nervous glance, uncertain whether he was calling her bluff or not.

'What sort of proof?'

'The sort of proof which will convict him.'

'I don't believe you.'

'He was seen on my boat last night,' he said.

'So?'

He gave her a hard look. 'My boat is now at the bottom of Parsley Bay.'

'I hardly see that someone stepping on to a boat immediately makes them responsible for sinking it,' she said. 'Or at least not someone with the small body mass index of my brother.'

'Very funny.' His eyes challenged hers.

'What about fingerprints?' she asked. 'Got any of those?'

He held her look for far longer than she would have liked.

'I'm sure you know fingerprints are a little difficult to find when a boat has been submerged for several hours.'

'What a shame,' she said without sincerity.

'But—' he deliberately paused for effect '—your brother did oblige me by leaving a calling card.' He took something out of the breast pocket of his shirt and held it up for her to see.

Maddison swallowed.

'Recognise this?' he asked.

For endless seconds she stared at the sterling silver surf chain she'd given Kyle for his eighteenth birthday.

'No,' she lied.

'You're predictable if nothing else.' He pocketed the chain once more.

'That chain could belong to anybody,' she pointed out.

'Anybody, that is, with the initials KBJ,' he put in neatly. 'What does the B stand for, by the way?'

'None of your business.'

'While we're on the subject of names, what is yours?'

'That's also none of your business.'

'I'm making it my business.'

She didn't care for the implacable threat in his tone but she knew there was little she could do to stop him finding out everything he needed to know and more. He quite clearly knew too much as it was and it made her increasingly uneasy.

She lowered her gaze after a lengthy silence and muttered, 'My name is Maddison.'

'Maddison.' His tongue caressed her name and she gave a little involuntary shiver of reaction. 'It suits you.'

He stepped away from her and she let out her breath in relief. She watched him as he wandered about her small sitting room, stopping to pick up a book from the coffee table as if he owned the place. She had to admit he had an incredible air of authority about him. She imagined it came from his considerable wealth; no doubt he was used to calling all the shots. His height, too, only added to that authority, as did his immaculate mode of dress. Designer suits, she decided, could have no better hanger than the leanly muscled frame which spoke of a man who obviously enjoyed and played a lot of sport. A broad chest, lean waist tapering to even leaner hips and long hard thighs beneath. His thick, closely cropped curly hair was as black as the ace of spades and his eyes were intelligent and astute, his mouth firm but full enough to hint at a brooding sensuality. His jaw was shadowed as if shaving once a day was not quite enough, which only added to the aura of unmistakable masculinity that oozed from each and every pore of his body. He caught her eyes on him as he turned to look at her.

'Maddison Jones, I have a bargain to drive with you.'

'What sort of bargain?' Her tone was suspicious.

He put the book he was holding down before answering.

'As you can imagine the loss of my yacht has incurred considerable expense.'

'What sort of expense?' she asked cautiously.

His dark eyes held hers.

'One point five million dollars, to be exact.'

She couldn't disguise her indrawn breath in time. 'Oh, my God!'

'Yes, I said as much at the time,' he admitted wryly, 'Or at least words to that effect.'

She could just imagine the sort of words he might have used.

'I don't see what this has to do with me.'

'It has everything to do with you, especially since you're so determined to protect your brother.'

'What do you mean?'

He gave her a leisurely look.

'Since you're so obviously lying to cover Kyle's tracks, I guess that leaves me with no choice but to deal directly with you.'

'I can't pay back that amount of money.'

'Not many people can,' he agreed. 'But that's not to say you couldn't in your own inimitable way redress the balance.'

'I can't imagine what you're getting at.'

'I'm offering you a position, Miss Jones.' He smiled seductively and then added smokily, 'Maddison.'

She gritted her teeth against the sound of her name on his lips.

'What sort of position?'

'The sort of position most women would clutch at with both hands.'

'I'm afraid I'm not quite up to date on what most women would do for the simple reason I am not most women.'

'You surprise me, Maddison. I had you picked as an opportunist, not unlike your father and brother.'

'My father did nothing wrong.'

He inclined his head.

'I respect your very obvious loyalty but your father proved his guilt by bowing under the pressure of accusation.'

'An accusation that was uncalled for and totally false!' she retorted hotly.

'It's understandable you would cling to that view but I have reason to believe otherwise.'

'You wouldn't recognise the truth if it jumped out of your over-stuffed wallet.'

'I beg to differ, Miss Jones. I have a great understanding of the truth. What remains to be seen is whether you do as well.'

'You can't make a criminal out of my brother.'

'I can and I will if I have to,' he assured her. 'But for the time being I'm prepared to suspend my judgement on your brother as long as you do what I suggest.'

'I can't imagine what scheme you have in mind,' she said scathingly.

'Can't you?'

She gave him an icy look. 'No doubt it has your unscrupulous desires at its centre.'

'Desire is a very good choice of word.' He smiled. 'I like the sound of that.'

Maddison didn't like the tone of his voice; it seemed to suggest a growing intimacy between them she didn't want to acknowledge in any shape or form.

'What do you want from me?' she asked. 'I have no money worth speaking of and I think I've made it more than clear I have no intention of revealing the whereabouts of my brother. What else is there?'

He took his time answering. She was intently conscious of his lazy surveillance, the fine hairs on the back of her neck rising in reaction to his studied gaze.

'I think you might prove to be very useful to me,' he said. 'Very useful indeed.'

'I can't imagine what you mean.' She sent him another nervous glance.

'I have a proposition to make.'

'What sort of proposition?'

'The sort of proposition that will clear your brother of all charges, wipe his slate clean, if you like.'

A flicker of hope burned and died in her breast within seconds. She didn't trust him; he had all the aces in his hand and he would throw them on the table at any moment, she was sure.

'Just how far are you prepared to go to protect your brother?' he asked after another tight little pause.

'As far as it takes.' She lifted her chin a fraction.

His smile didn't quite reach his eyes. 'As far as having a relationship with me?'

She held his direct look without speaking, her heart skipping a beat in her chest.

'I need the smokescreen of a new alliance. You could prove to be very useful in my current circumstances.'

'I can't imagine how.' She finally found her voice.

'I need a cover,' he said. 'I have a situation, so to speak; I need an alibi, the ironclad sort.'

'I don't think I can help you.'

'On the contrary, I think you can. I want you to pretend to be my current mistress. How would you feel about that?'

'Do you want the truth or politeness?'

'Both.'

'Well—' she tilted her head at him '—for a start I would never allow myself to be your mistress.'

'What about as my wife?'

'That's even more unlikely.'

'What about if you had no choice?'

She gave him an arctic look. 'I would always have a choice.'

'Not if your brother's freedom depended on it.'

Maddison felt cornered and she was sure he was aware of it.

'What do you mean?' she asked, trying to buy time.

'It's easy.' He gave her an unreadable look. 'I can call Kyle's probation officer right now to tell him he's flown the coop, or you can agree to do a favour for me, simple as that.'

'You want me to pretend to be your wife?'

'No.' He shook his head. 'I've changed my mind. I have much more specific plans for you.'

She gave him a blank stare. 'I don't think I'm following you.'

'I don't want you to pretend anything,' he said smoothly. 'I want you to actually be my wife.'

Her mouth dropped open in shock. 'You can't possibly mean that!'

'In time, Maddison Jones, you will come to learn that I mean everything I say.'

She could well believe it, but didn't want to add to his already monumental ego by expressing it verbally.

'You surely can't expect me to agree to this outrageous proposal,' she said instead.

'I think I've made it clear what will happen if you don't,' he answered. 'Kyle will find himself in a four-by-four cell, playing cards with who knows what unsavoury inmates.'

She closed her eyes against the image his words conjured. Her brother was wilful and wayward, but he didn't deserve imprisonment, and she would do everything in her power to stop it happening.

'I...I need some time to think about this.' She avoided his eyes.

'I'll give you a week, no more.'

'*A week?*'

He gave a single nod. 'But, let me warn you, I'll be following your every move, so if you have any plans to escape, forget them.'

He reached into his back pocket and handed her a business card. She took it with nerveless fingers and stared at it sightlessly for a long moment.

'You can reach me on that number when you've made your decision,' he informed her. 'I'll tell my secretary to expect your call by five p.m. on Monday.'

She wished she had the courage to tear the card into a thousand pieces, and if it hadn't been for Kyle she would have, but instead she closed her palm around it, feeling its sharp edges digging into her flesh like an instrument of torture. She lifted her gaze back to his unwavering one, the cold fingertips of fear edging their way up her spine at the self-satisfied gleam reflected in his black-hooded eyes.

'I'm assuming from all this that your boat wasn't adequately insured,' she said.

'It was very adequately insured,' he informed her. 'But this is my way of ensuring I get the best possible return.'

The predatory look he gave her caused her stomach to turn over unexpectedly.

'You're taking a very big risk; you don't know where I might have been or who I've been with.' She was deliberately provocative, even though she had never been so close to a man until he'd stepped into her personal space a few minutes ago.

'I have no real interest in your sexual proclivities,' he said dismissively. 'This will not be a real lasting marriage.'

'It's to be temporary?' She clutched at the life-line hopefully.

'Of course.' His eyes glinted darkly. 'Isn't every marriage?'

She didn't have it in her to argue the point, even if she'd wanted to. She'd read the latest figures on marital success and they weren't all that promising.

'Aren't you worried I might take you to the cleaners at the end of our...arrangement?' she asked.

'Not at all. By the time our marriage is annulled you'll be very much aware of what sort of outcome such an action would produce.'

She lifted her chin at the thinly veiled threat behind his words.

'Do I have your word the marriage would stay in name only?'

'I can assure you, Maddison, my physical needs are being very satisfactorily catered for elsewhere. I have absolutely no interest in chasing you around the bedroom. You will be able to sleep in peace.'

She knew it was highly inconsistent of her to be annoyed by his callous dismissal of her attractiveness to the opposite sex; she knew she was hardly model material but surely she wasn't ready for the shelf yet?

'So, if I agree to this arrangement it is safe to assume I'm to turn a blind eye to your activities for appearance's sake?'

'You will not only turn a blind eye, you will do everything in your power to maintain the illusion of a happy union whenever we are in public, which means, of course, the same freedom I enjoy will not be available to you.'

'Meaning?'

'Meaning any dalliances you might be tempted to conduct will have to be temporarily shelved until such time as our marriage is over.'

'So you can have your cake and eat it too, but I must not?'

'That's correct.'

'That's archaic!'

'That's the deal, take it or leave it.'

She longed to tell him what to do with his preposterous proposal but a vision of her brother in handcuffs flitted unbidden into her mind and she snapped her mouth shut.

'Don't forget, Maddison, I'm doing you a very big favour here. One point five million dollars is a huge debt for someone in your position to pay. This way the debt can be cleared within a short space of time. Your brother can stop looking over his shoulder and you can walk away with a clear conscience knowing you saved him from a fate thought to be worse than death.'

'What sort of time-frame are you thinking of?' she asked, her insides twisting painfully.

He pursed his lips for a moment in a gesture of deep thought.

'At a guess I'd give it six months. Any longer and you might be tempted to get a little too attached to the role.'

'You must be joking.' She gave him a scathing glance.

'One can never be too sure,' he said with another one of his secret smiles. 'Women have rather an annoying habit of becoming clingy at times.'

'It must be your money,' she shot back. 'It can't possibly have anything whatsoever to do with your personality.'

His sudden laughter surprised her; it had a deep masculine sound to it that sent an arrow of sensation up her back as if he'd reached out and touched her with his long fingers. It made her feel as if she'd inadvertently uncovered an even more dangerous facet to him, the ability to slip under her defences and catch her off guard.

'Maddison Jones—' his eyes twinkled with lingering amusement as he surveyed her mutinous features '—I'm looking forward to hearing your decision next week. I think our little arrangement could prove to be very entertaining, very entertaining indeed.'

Before she could think of a suitably stinging reply the door opened under his hand and he was gone, leaving her standing there with his business card tightly clenched in her hand.

She opened her palm and winced when she saw the tiny pinprick of blood one of the sharp edges had drawn from her soft flesh. She couldn't help wondering if it were some sort of omen, or perhaps a warning specifically aimed at her; if she were to allow herself to get too close to someone like Demetrius Papasakis she would be, in the end, the only one to get hurt.

CHAPTER TWO

MADDISON had never known a week to go so quickly. As each day unfolded her panic grew steadily inside her until she began to feel as if she were on death row, waiting for the next cock's crow to herald her imminent demise.

She hadn't wasted the time available to her but had tried everything in her power to extricate herself from the clutches of Demetrius Papasakis—to no avail. As if to deliberately intensify her desperate circumstances, she had received a flood of bills in the space of days, one of which was a hefty speeding fine of her brother's which she knew he wouldn't be able to pay.

She spent a miserable weekend trying to think of a way out of her difficulties but in the end had to admit she was well and truly trapped. Her modest income from the second hand bookstore where she worked would hardly cover Kyle's speeding ticket let alone a million-and-a-half dollar boat.

However, when she arrived at the bookstore on the Monday morning she received an even bigger shock. Her boss, Hugo McGill, looked at her over the top of his reading glasses, his white whiskers moving up and down restively.

'Maddison, I have some unfortunate news.'

Cold dread trickled into her stomach at his ominous tone.

'What's wrong?' she asked, not sure she really wanted to know.

'I'm afraid I'm selling up.'

She blinked at him for a second or two. 'This is rather sudden, isn't it?'

'Yes and no,' he answered. 'I've wanted a change for ages but I felt I should wait until I got a good price for the place. I had an offer at the weekend and, to put it rather bluntly, it was too good to refuse.'

She sat back in her chair as the realisation of her circumstances dawned. 'I suppose the new owner has no plans to keep the business running?'

'No,' he said. 'The building is going to be demolished to make way for a hotel.'

'A hotel?' She gaped at him.

'A luxury one,' Hugo said proudly as if somehow that made it better. 'The fruit shop and the bakery have been sold as well to make room for it.'

Maddison had never felt so angry in all her twenty-four years. She knew without asking who was behind this sudden redevelopment plan but a perverse desire to hear her boss articulate the name urged her on.

'Do you happen to know who's behind this purchase?'

'Yes, the Greek billionaire, Demetrius Papasakis. He was in the papers at the weekend over the loss of his boat. Did you happen to see it?'

'No.' She shifted her gaze uncomfortably. 'I didn't have time to look at the papers.'

'It seems his luxury yacht was sabotaged one night last week.'

'Did he say who he suspected of doing it?' she asked, carefully avoiding his eye.

'Not in so many words, but he did say he had the matter in hand. I feel sorry for whoever did it, to tell you the truth. Demetrius Papasakis is not the sort of enemy I would go out of my way to attract.'

'I'm sure there are lots of people who would agree with you,' she answered wryly.

'He's got an edge of cold ruthlessness about him,' Hugo continued. 'But I suppose when he's got that amount of money who's going to challenge him?'

'Who indeed?'

'Anyway, I'm sorry about your job. You've been a good girl, Maddison. I'll write you a decent reference and if I hear of anything you might be interested in I'll call you. I know it's terribly short notice but business is business as they say.'

She gave him a wan smile as she pushed in the chair she'd been sitting on. 'Yes, it certainly is.'

Maddison had six hours to get through before she announced her decision. She glanced at her watch repeatedly, her heart hammering with every passing minute as she thought about the phone call she had to make by five p.m.

She left the bookshop at four-thirty, surprising herself at her detached attitude as she walked away from it without a backward glance. She searched for a public telephone at four-forty-five, but each one she came to was out of order. She stood on yet another street corner and nibbled at the rough edge of a fingernail as she thought about what to do. In the end she decided a phone call was the cowardly thing to do, that the best way to approach the situation was head on. She wasn't going to relay her message to Demetrius Papasakis via his secretary; she was going to have it out with him face-to-face.

She rummaged in her bag for the business card he'd given her and quickly memorised the address of his office tower, relieved to find she had just enough time to get there on foot if she hurried. She arrived somewhat breathlessly outside the imposing building in the north of the city, her hair sticking to the back of her neck and her white blouse clinging to her back where beads of nervous perspiration had collected. She brushed an errant strand out of her face and stabbed her finger at the call button of the lifts, trying to ignore the distinct flutter of unease in her belly.

The lift swept her up to the administration floor where she encountered a middle-aged woman guarding the reception desk.

'Can I help you?' the woman asked in a haughty tone.

Maddison brushed another wayward strand out of her face.

'I'm here to see Mr Papasakis.'

'Do you have an appointment?'

'No, not really. I was supposed to call him, but at the last minute I decided to come in person. My name is Maddison Jones.'

The woman's eyes swept over her. 'You're Miss Jones?'

'That's correct.' Maddison lifted her chin in a token gesture of pride.

She didn't care for the look the secretary was giving her, as if she was the last person anyone would expect Demetrius Papasakis to be associated with. She suffered no illusions about her out-of-date clothes and scuffed shoes, but she knew her figure was nothing to be ashamed of, even if her hair needed brushing and her lips a touch of gloss.

'I'll let him know you're here.' The woman reached for the intercom on her desk.

'Thank you,' Maddison responded politely.

She heard the deep burr of Demetrius's voice on the machine as she stood waiting, and glancing at the clock on the wall saw the second hand tick down the remaining seconds—ten, nine, eight, seven...

'He'll see you now,' the woman said, interrupting her quiet panic.

She followed the woman's directions to his office and gave the solid door one small sharp knock.

'Come.'

She opened the door and her eyes immediately went to his seated figure behind the huge expanse of his desk.

He got to his feet with languid grace and greeted her. 'Maddison, and right on time too.'

She didn't answer but stood in front of his desk with a fiery look in her clear blue gaze.

Demetrius couldn't help feeling faintly amused. She was so touchingly defiant, pretending she wasn't intimidated when she very clearly was. It intrigued him in a way. Most of the women he'd been involved with would have jumped at the chance to wear his ring and yet here she was looking as if he'd asked her to walk the plank above an ocean full of sharks.

He indicated the chair for her to sit on with a sweep of his hand.

'Please, take a seat.'

'I'd rather stand,' she said through stiff lips.

'As you wish.' He sat back down and picked up a pen off his desk and gave it a click. 'Have you come to a decision regarding my proposal?'

'I'm surprised you still have the gall to call it a proposal,' she said. 'I would prefer the term blackmail.'

'Blackmail is a strong word.' He gave his pen another audible click. 'I'd like to remind you now that you can walk out of that door at any point and accept the consequences.'

She tightened her spine at his chilling warning.

'But you've made it impossible for me to do so, haven't you?' She eyeballed him directly.

'I take it you're referring to my real estate dealings over the weekend?' He leant back in his chair and propped his feet on his desk in an indolent pose that made the blood simmer in her veins.

'You did it deliberately, didn't you? To flush me out like a rat down a drainpipe.'

'Not quite the metaphor I would have chosen, but it will suffice, I suppose.'

'You're totally sick!'

'I'll take that as a "no" then?' His dark gaze glinted with lazy amusement.

She clenched and unclenched her fists in an effort to keep control.

'I'm going to make you a promise, Mr Papasakis, one that I hope you won't forget.'

'You intrigue me.' The corner of his mouth lifted sardonically. 'Pray tell me what delightful pledge you have in store.'

Her eyes flashed with fire. 'I will marry you, but you will live to regret it; I'm going to make absolutely certain of that.'

He lifted his feet off the desk in one easy movement and stood up, straightening to his full height as he came around the desk to her side. She stood her ground determinedly, but on the inside she was shaking and was sure he was aware of it.

'You and whose army?' He reached out and touched her flaming cheek with one idle finger.

She jerked her head out of his reach and glared up at him.

'Mock me all you like but I'll be the one laughing in the end,' she promised.

'How absolutely terrifying you are when aroused.'

'I'm not aroused!' She stamped her foot at him. 'I'm angry, blindingly so!'

'Come now, Maddison.' He caught her upper arms with his hands and held her gently but firmly. 'Why not give in with good grace? You'll be the envy of single women everywhere. A rich husband, all the clothes and trinkets you want in exchange for a few months of your time. What more could you ask?'

'I could ask for a lot more in a husband,' she threw at him coldly. 'Being tied to an unprincipled playboy is not my idea of nuptial bliss, nor is the prospect of being a laughing stock when you carry on with your perfidious behaviour behind my back.'

'It won't be behind your back,' he said. 'I've already informed you of the terms of our agreement.'

'Your double standards make me sick!'

'No doubt they are a little distasteful, but that's the deal. I can't have people wondering why my wife is having a bit on the side; it's not good for my reputation.'

'I can't believe your arrogance,' she spat.

His hands on her arms tightened momentarily.

'I also can't have my wife calling me names, is that understood?'

She met his implacable look with defiance. 'I won't be your wife for long.'

'No, but while you are you'll do as you're told.'

She gritted her teeth against the string of invectives on her tongue.

'You'd much rather be my temporary wife than see your brother go to prison, wouldn't you?' he added when she didn't speak.

'I'd much rather like to see *you* rot in prison,' she ground out.

'Answer me, Maddison.' He tilted her chin to meet his eyes. 'Tell me how much you'd rather be married to me than see your brother's future go up in smoke.'

She hadn't thought it was possible to hate another person so much as she did him at that moment. Her blood thrummed with it, thundering in her ears as she felt every last remnant of her pride being stripped away by his ruthlessness.

'I…I don't want to see Kyle go to prison,' she bit out.

'And the rest?'

'And…and I'd rather be your temporary…wife.'

He smiled one of his hateful smiles and her palm itched to wipe it from his face. He lowered his mouth towards hers in a slow motion movement which should have been enough warning for her to get out of the way but somehow wasn't. She closed her eyes as his lips connected with hers, surprised at how warm and dry they felt as they brushed along hers. Her lips clung to his, her mouth opening to the heated probe of his tongue as he traced the line of her bottom lip in spine-weakening intimacy. She felt the slight graze of his teeth as he took her bottom lip between them, holding her for a heart-stopping moment until releasing her, only to dive between the soft folds of her lips to taste her completely. She felt the unmistakable thrust of his hard thighs between her quivering ones, felt too the evidence of his essential maleness as he leaned into her softness.

He lifted his head a fraction and her eyes sprang open to see him watching her steadily, his own dark gaze inscrutable.

'I'll be in contact with you over the arrangements.' He stepped away from her.

She watched him silently as he returned to the chair behind his desk, irritated beyond measure at his calm indifference to what had passed between them in that one brief kiss.

'Under the circumstances I thought it would be best if we have a small ceremony,' he added. 'Is there anyone you'd particularly like to invite?'

'Apart from a sniper, do you mean?'

His eyes held hers for a lengthy pause.

'Careful, Maddison, you're supposed to be in love with me, remember? Not planning my demise behind my back.'

'I could never be in love with you. You're everything I most detest in a man.'

'All I'm asking you to do is pretend.'

'It's going to take every bit of acting ability I possess to do so.'

'I don't care what it takes as long as you do it. Otherwise you know the score.'

'I suppose you're going to hang that threat over my head for as long as our marriage continues?'

'Think of it as my insurance policy,' he said. 'I'll let your brother off the hook if and when I feel you've done what is required.'

'Am I to be allowed to contact him?'

'I can hardly stop you,' he said. 'Besides, you'll have to tell him of our impending marriage for no doubt he'll read about it in the papers.'

'How am I going to explain our sudden marriage to him?'

'You're a woman. Think of a suitable lie to put him off the scent.'

'Your view of my gender positively reeks of misogyny.'

'No doubt it does, but then in my thirty-four years I have yet to meet a woman who doesn't run true to form.'

A small frown settled between her brows at his words. She wondered if somewhere along the line he'd been hurt by a woman, perhaps one who had got the upper hand with him and rubbed his nose in it.

'I'll arrange for some legal papers to be sent to you for your perusal,' he said, cutting across her thoughts. 'As for wedding finery, I'll organise a credit card for you; it should be available in three or four days.'

'I'm to be a real bride?' She stared at him in alarm.

'What's wrong? Do you have a thing about wearing white?'

'No.' If only he knew the irony of his words, she thought.

'I just didn't expect you to want to go to so much trouble over a temporary arrangement.'

'It's only temporary to us,' he pointed out. 'To everyone else this must be presented as a match made in heaven. If we have some hole-and-corner ceremony it won't look good enough to believe. Besides, everyone knows how Greek men pride themselves on scoring a virginal bride.'

Hot colour suffused her cheeks.

'I hope being a virgin isn't part of your stipulations?'

'I'm not so stupid as to imagine you've got to the age you are without experiencing sex first hand. I take it I'm right?'

'Of course,' she lied.

'That's all for now.' He got to his feet, effectively dismissing her. 'I'll be in touch.'

'Is that all?'

'Was there something else?' He glanced at his watch before meeting her incensed gaze across the desk.

'No.' She snapped her mouth over the single word and snatched up her bag from the floor.

She was at the door with her hand on the knob when his voice halted her.

'I wouldn't advise any last minute countermoves. Remember I'm watching you.'

'How could I forget?' she tossed back at him before closing the door behind her.

She was halfway down the corridor when a heady cloying perfume began to assault her nostrils. She looked up to see an exotic-looking dark-haired woman sashaying past her towards Demetrius's office, her clinging black dress outlining her very generous curves.

'Is Demetrius free now?' the woman asked in a kittenish tone which sickened Maddison to her stomach.

Some spark of residual defiance made Maddison adopt an equally provocative pose as she faced his latest conquest.

'I hope I haven't worn him out too much for you,' she purred suggestively. 'He's quite something when he's all fired up.'

The woman's dark brows snapped together irritably. 'That low-down bastard's been having it off with you?' she shrieked.

Maddison smoothed down her skirt before straightening her crumpled blouse.

'He's insatiable, but then I expect you already know that.' She batted her eyelashes and then, leaning towards the spitting other woman, murmured conspiratorially, 'I've heard a rumour he's getting married. I'd be careful if I were you—jealous wives are the pits, aren't they?'

The woman's eyes narrowed in anger and she spun away to click-clack down the hall towards Demetrius's office on heels that Maddison was sure were going to end up in his back at some point if the woman's expression was anything to go by.

She smiled a little cat's smile and continued on her way towards the exit. It felt good to have the upper hand just for once, and she was going to enjoy every single delicious minute.

On Wednesday morning a courier arrived at her apartment with a sheaf of papers and an envelope containing a credit card with her name on it.

She sat on her old sofa and went over the papers in detail. They were fairly straightforward, citing the date and time of their intended marriage and the conditions were laid out in simple terms. By signing, she was immediately relinquishing any financial rights normally afforded a marital partner on the dissolution of their marriage. She signed it with considerable relish; she didn't want his stinking money anyway.

She wasn't sure what to do about the credit card however. She had no savings left after Kyle's airfare and traffic infringement, and although Hugo had given her severance pay she still had to finalise the electricity and phone bills before the end of the week, but even so she felt distinctly uncomfortable spending Demetrius's money. In the end she decided to mail it back to him, not even bothering to write a covering note to accompany it.

As much as it galled her to have to do so she knew she couldn't leave it too many more days without contacting him.

She had one or two questions to ask regarding their living arrangements once they were married; somehow she didn't think he'd agree to move into her tiny apartment with the peeling paint and constantly flickering light bulbs.

He wasn't available to speak to her when she called his office, which instantly annoyed her. She didn't want to wait around holding her breath for him to return her calls, but neither did she want to be left in a state of indecision and uncertainty over whatever arrangements he'd made.

Her hand hovered over the telephone later that evening as she fought with herself over whether to call his private number or not. Before her finger had pressed the first digit, however, the doorbell of her apartment pealed and she put the handset down with a clatter as she got to her feet to answer it.

Demetrius was standing there with a small smile lurking about the corners of his mouth. 'Hello, Maddison.' His dark eyes swept over her fluffy tracksuit before returning to her face. 'Pleased to see me?'

She stepped aside for him to come in.

'So nice of you to return my calls in person,' she said. 'I'm surprised you can afford the time. Haven't you got a hot date tonight?'

'I wonder you can ask that,' he said with a tiny glimmer of amusement in his eyes. 'Especially when you deliberately sabotaged my relationship with Elena Tsoulis.'

'If she was so easily put off by me you're definitely underselling yourself,' she returned.

'Perhaps you're right.' He shrugged himself out of his suit jacket and hung it over the back of the sofa. 'She was close to her use by date anyway.'

She inwardly seethed at his callous attitude.

He turned to face her, his hand going to his tie to loosen it. 'What did you want to see me about?'

'I want to know what to do about my apartment.'

He swept the room with an ironic glance. 'You call this an apartment?'

'No,' she said, stung by his disdain. 'I call it home.'

'Well then, to borrow your own words, you're definitely underselling yourself.'

'It's all I can afford.'

'No doubt because you've been so busy bailing your brother out of trouble all the time. You should be a little more selective in how you rescue him. He'll never learn to take responsibility with you stepping into the breach all the time.'

'It's none of your business what I do for my brother.'

'I beg to differ. I now have a vested interest in how you help your brother. One could argue, in fact, that it will be my money that will be used to support him if the need should arise.'

'I'm going to get another job as soon as I can.'

'There's no need for you to do so immediately,' he said. 'I quite fancy the idea of a kept woman.'

'I'd rather die.'

'Such strong words,' he chided. 'No, I definitely like the idea of you at my beck and call every hour of the day.'

'You will soon tire of it.'

He grinned at her disarmingly. 'I wonder.'

She turned away from the contemplative look in his eye.

'I wanted to talk to you about living arrangements,' she said.

'Ah, yes—' he sat on the sofa and stretched out his long legs in front of him '—the living arrangements. I was wondering when we'd come to that.'

'I'm assuming you want me to live with you?'

'Of course.'

'But what about my apartment?'

'Get rid of it.'

She took a turn about the room in agitation.

'What's the problem, Maddison?' he asked her. 'Surely you're not balking at the idea of sharing my penthouse?'

She turned back to face him. 'Where do you live?'

'In the Papasakis Park View Tower Hotel.'

'You live in a hotel?' She looked at him incredulously.

'Why not?' He crossed his ankles. 'The beds are comfortable, the food edible, and the showers hot. Why wouldn't I live there?'

'I would've thought a man of your means would have a castle of his own,' she said. 'It must be very impersonal living in a hotel all the time.'

'I'm used to it. Anyway, I'm in and out of the country such a lot I haven't got time to manage a private residence.'

'How much travelling do you do?'

He gave her a knowing look. 'I can see where your mind is headed. If you think you can get away with anything while my back is turned you can think again. I might be out of the country rather regularly but I keep a steady eye on what's happening when I'm away.'

'I wasn't thinking anything of the sort,' she lied. 'I was just wondering what I should do when you're away, that's all.'

He propped his hands behind his head and surveyed her casually. 'You'll be too busy pretending to be the devoted wife in my absence and if you behave yourself I might even allow you to come with me occasionally.'

'I can't wait.'

He laughed at the insincerity of her tone. 'Come on, Maddison, you do your sex a disservice to insist your motives are all above board. What young woman wouldn't want an all expenses paid trip overseas?'

'I would prefer to have more choice over my travelling partner.'

'Be that as it may, I still think you should be grateful I've been so obliging in all this. Another man might have asked you to pay back every cent.'

'I would rather work an eighteen hour day for the rest of my life than spend an hour with you.'

His expression closed over and she wondered if she'd pressed one too many of his buttons.

'You have a lamentable lack of grace in your choice of words,' he said. 'One would hope that tendency will abate as time goes on.'

'You expect me to be grateful to you for blackmailing me into this arrangement?'

'No.' He got to his feet with languid ease. 'I don't expect you to be grateful; I expect you to be realistic. Your brother is a prison statistic waiting to happen. I'm giving you a chance to redeem his future prospects.'

'What do you want from me?'

'I thought I'd made that clear. I want you to pretend to be a wife in love for a short period of time.'

'I'm not sure I'm up to the task.'

'Then you'd better brush up on your skills,' he said. 'If you don't, the weight of the law will fall about your brother's shoulders.'

'That threat is going to wear out if you brandish it about too much.'

'It's not a threat, Maddison, it's a promise, and if you don't fulfil your side of the bargain, neither will I.'

'I don't know why you've targeted me as your victim in all this,' she said. 'I have absolutely nothing to offer you.'

'You have everything to offer me,' he countered. 'You love your brother and are prepared to do anything to save him. That sort of loyalty is not to be disregarded.'

'You're exploiting it for your own ends.'

'Maybe, but at the end of the day you're the one who wins in all this.'

'How so?'

'Your brother will be released from all retribution from me, and you'll be adequately compensated for your time and efforts in portraying yourself as a devoted wife. I can't do any more than that.'

'I still think there's a loophole in all of this.'

'It's understandable you'd see it that way, but let me reassure you I have no such motive. I wish only for a quick solution to my own problems, and as it turns out you are a very convenient alibi.'

'It's been all too convenient for you, though, hasn't it?' she asked. 'My brother has played right into your hands.'

'Your brother was foolish enough to leave a footprint. If he hadn't done so I would still be scouring the streets for the culprit.'

'I only wish my brother had thought to torch your car and your hotel as well,' she said bitterly.

His mouth thinned as he took in her enraged features. 'That would have been most inadvisable. If he had done so you would not be marrying me next week, and your useless brother would be facing me in court.'

Maddison didn't have an answer at the ready.

'I would advise you, Maddison, to see things as they are. You stand in front of your brother's freedom; don't throw it away on a whim of petulance directed at me.'

'I hate you.'

'I'm very glad you do,' he said. 'I wouldn't like to think you harboured any other emotion considering the terms I've laid down.'

'How can you sleep at night?' she asked.

'I can sleep with ease,' he said. 'Knowing that I did all I could to secure my own interests.'

'At the expense of someone else's?'

'Yes,' he said without apology. 'At the expense of someone else's.'

She turned away from his arrogant features and sucked in a steadying breath. 'How soon do you wish to activate this fake marriage?'

'Next week.'

She swung back to face him, her expression full of alarm. '*Next week?*' She had forgotten it would be so soon.

He gave a casual lift of one shoulder as if they were merely discussing the date of a picnic, not a legally binding agreement such as marriage.

'I thought it best to get the deed over with as quickly as possible. A whirlwind affair will attract exactly the sort of press attention I need to divert attention away from my other activities.'

'How can anyone possibly organise a wedding in a week?'

He gave her an imperious smile as he tapped his inside pocket. 'That over-stuffed wallet you referred to before comes in rather handy when I want something done in a hurry.'

'I just bet it does.' She gave him a caustic glance.

'I also thought we should spend some time together this week,' he added. 'It will give credibility to our relationship if we're seen in public a few times.'

'I'm busy this week.'

'Cancel.'

'I don't want to.'

'You might think it amusing to defy me at every turn, but let me assure you, Maddison, I will always maintain the upper hand. You will accompany me on several dates this week and demonstrate your ecstatic enjoyment in being in my company. Is that clear?'

Mutiny flared in her eyes as she faced him. 'I'll loathe every minute.'

'So will your brother if he ends up in jail.'

Blue eyes clashed with black until Maddison had no choice but to look away.

She heard him shrug himself into his jacket and the jangle of his keys as he searched for them in his trouser pocket but she didn't turn around.

'I'll call for you tomorrow. Be ready at seven.'

'What will I wear?' she asked stiffly.

She heard him open the door but still refused to face him.

'Surprise me,' he said and closed the door behind him.

Maddison couldn't help smiling a mischievous little smile as she listened to his footsteps fade away as he strode down the stairs to his car. Demetrius Papasakis was in for a surprise all right; she would have the last word and the last mocking laugh as well.

CHAPTER THREE

THE telephone rang just as Maddison was going through her wardrobe in preparation for the following evening. She absentmindedly reached down to answer the bedroom extension as she dangled a pair of bright red fishnets from one hand.

'Maddison?' Kyle's voice sounded out after the long-distance pips. 'Is that you?'

'Kyle!' She tossed the stockings to one side as she sat on the bed. 'How are you?'

'I'm sunburnt, saddle-sore and constantly starving, but I'm fine.'

'Aren't they feeding you properly?'

'Of course they are, but I've never been so active before. You'd never believe what I can put away.'

'I can believe it.' Her tone was dry. She'd been paying the grocery bills for months and suffered no illusions about her brother's capacity for consuming food. 'Are you enjoying the work?'

'I hate to admit it, but yes I am.' His tone was sheepish. 'I like the outdoor life, Maddy, and the Marquis family is great. I think I could really stick it out in the bush, maybe work the circuit a bit until I get some money behind me.'

Maddison could barely believe what she was hearing. Her restless younger brother hadn't stuck at a job for more than a day or two and here he was declaring his intention of staying in the outback for months. It made the sacrifice she was about to make marginally more worthwhile, in spite of her reservations about Demetrius Papasakis.

'I need to tell you something,' she began uncertainly. 'It's about Mr Papasakis.'

There was a tiny silence at the other end.

'What about him?'

'He knows you sank his boat.'

There was a telling silence for five heartbeats.

'But he doesn't know where I am, right?'

'No, but he's not really all that interested in where you are at present. He has other fish to fry.'

'You mean he's not going to come after me and press charges?' Relief had crept into Kyle's voice.

'Not unless things don't go according to plan.'

'What do you mean?'

'He's made a sort of pact with me on your behalf.'

'What sort of pact?'

'He's not going to press charges as long as I do what he says for a period of a few months.'

'He's blackmailing you?'

Maddison heard the unmistakable convulsive swallow in his throat. 'You could call it that.'

'Oh my God; it's all my fault.' It was the first time she had heard any sort of remorse in her brother's voice and a part of her had to admit that perhaps some good might eventually come out of this bizarre arrangement.

'Don't worry,' she reassured him. 'I've got it in hand; I know how to deal with someone like Demetrius Papasakis.'

'What does he want you to do?'

'He wants me to marry him.'

'*Marry him?*' he gasped incredulously. 'Whatever for?'

A remnant of feminine pique niggled at her at his surprise that anyone, even a playboy like Demetrius Papasakis, would express any desire to tie himself to her.

'As far as I'm aware I haven't cracked any mirrors lately,' she said somewhat tartly.

'I didn't mean it like that.' Kyle was instantly apologetic. 'I mean why would he want to marry at all? He's not the marrying type.'

'He needs a smokescreen relationship,' she informed him. 'Or so he told me. I'm to be the happy wife at home to provide him with a suitable alibi while he cavorts with whoever he likes.'

'And you're OK with that?'

'I don't have any choice. When you sank that boat my freedom went with it to the bottom of the harbour.'

'I'm so sorry, Maddy. I'll make it up to you. I'll work hard and get us a place out here in the country where he can't find us.'

'I'm not going to run away from someone like Demetrius Papasakis,' she said determinedly. 'I'm going to stay and fight it out.'

'You're awesome, sis, do you know that?'

Maddison smiled at the admiration in her brother's tone.

'You ain't seen nothing yet, bro,' she said. 'You ain't seen nothing yet.'

At six-thirty the following evening Maddison stood in front of the full length mirror behind her bedroom door and inspected her ensemble.

She'd rummaged through her wardrobe for the outfit she'd worn to a friend's Pimps and Prostitutes Ball a couple of years ago. The short tight black PVC skirt and over the knee black boots with the garish fishnets were a perfect foil for the three sizes too small skimpy black top which was being somewhat overshadowed by the magnificent efforts of her lacy push-up bra.

Her make-up was the final touch—bright red lipstick, smudged of course, and heavy electric-blue eye-shadow and thick kohl pencil around her eyes giving her a distinctly raccoon-like look.

She gave herself a wicked grin; she looked like an absolute tart.

The doorbell rang at seven on the dot and, ignoring the slight flutter of last-minute nerves, she tottered over the threadbare carpet to answer it.

Demetrius didn't even flinch when he saw her.

'Ready?'

With the wind definitely taken out of her sails she had no choice but to nod her assent and follow him out to the car.

'Where are we going?' she asked once they were in the sleek black Jaguar.

'I thought I might surprise you,' he said, backing out of the car parking space.

She pursed her painted lips and wondered if she'd exactly been wise in trying to get the upper hand. She was beginning to suspect he was a whole lot more ruthless than she'd first allowed.

Her instincts had been right, she decided a short while later, when he parked in the main drag of the red light district of Kings Cross.

She gave him a nervous glance as he turned off the engine but his expression gave nothing away. She watched as he came around the bonnet of the car to open her door, his tall figure so striking in dark shirt and trousers that her stomach gave a funny flip flop as her door opened under his hand. She slid out with as much grace as her impossibly high heels allowed and stood uncertainly on the pavement, suddenly very conscious of the speculative looks she was receiving from the various pass-ers-by.

'There aren't any nice restaurants along here,' she said as he took her elbow to lead her down the street.

'I know.'

She stumbled over a broken bit of pavement and his hold tightened.

'Where are we going?' she asked.

'In here.'

He shepherded her into a seedy looking nightclub whose promotional signs promised scantily clad pole and lap dancers around the clock. Maddison felt the heat storm her cheeks as he propelled her to a table right up the front, her eyes instantly darting away from the buxom blonde cavorting with the slippery pole right near her chair.

'What would you like to drink?' Demetrius asked.

She swivelled in her seat to avoid the sight of a pair of breasts that without a doubt defied natural genetic construction.

'Anything,' she choked out.

The sleazy drinks waiter approached and, giving Maddison the once-over, asked for their order. She sat in a miserable silence as Demetrius asked for two champagne cocktails, her embarrassment increasing with every gyration of the dancer who seemed to be making a direct beeline for their table.

'How was your day?' Demetrius asked, leaning back in his chair.

'Fine.'

The dancer had quite clearly decided the most attractive man in the house was Demetrius, and she sidled up to trail a hand through his dark curly hair, shooting Maddison a challenging glance from beneath her fluttering, seductive lashes.

A seed of anger sprouted in her chest at how he'd swiftly turned the tables on her.

'This is a nice place,' she said perversely, taking a generous slug of her drink while trying to ignore the dancer's thigh, which was draped across Demetrius's knee.

'Yes, I thought you might feel right at home here,' he said, reaching for his drink.

'Do you come here often?' she asked.

'Not if I can help it.' He gave the dancer a sexy smile.

She could feel her blood boiling at his deliberate attempt to embarrass her and took another deep swig of her drink.

'Do they serve food here?' she asked once the dancer had moved on. 'I'm starving.'

'Finish your drink and I'll take you to Otto at Woolloomooloo Bay.'

It was impossible to think of a worse punishment, she decided, than to be taken to one of Sydney's premier restaurants dressed like a streetwalker. She had to admit that she'd seriously underestimated Demetrius Papasakis and quite clearly, for this evening at least, he'd claimed not only the last word but the last laugh as well.

She got to her feet and followed him out of the nightclub

with as much dignity as she could muster, but she knew the worst was probably still ahead of her.

It was.

The fine dining Otto offered in the refurbished wharf buildings at Woolloomooloo Bay was surpassed only by the elegant service and up-market clientele.

Maddison wished the floor would open up and let her sink to the harbour floor beneath, but it seemed Demetrius was after his pound of flesh and would stop at nothing to get it.

She was immediately conscious of the interested glances coming their way as they were led to their table, her embarrassment increasing a hundredfold to hear Demetrius addressed by name.

'Mr Papasakis, would you like to see the wine list?'

Demetrius leaned back as his napkin was laid across his lap.

'Don't bother,' he said. 'Just bring us the best champagne of the house. We're celebrating.'

The waiter had obviously been taught well for he didn't even raise a brow. 'Congratulations, Mr Papasakis,' he said. 'May I ask what the occasion is?'

'I'm getting married,' he said and smiled across at Maddison.

Maddison gave the waiter a wan smile and buried her head back in the menu.

'My hearty congratulations, sir. I hope you'll be very happy.'

Demetrius returned the waiter's smile with a self-satisfied one of his own. 'I intend to be very happy,' he said. 'Very happy indeed.'

Maddison waited until the waiter was out of earshot before she hissed across the table at him. 'Are you crazy? That man thinks you're marrying a prostitute! It will be all over the papers tomorrow.'

He leaned back in his chair and studied her in a leisurely manner. 'Isn't that what you intended?'

'No,' she snapped. 'I wanted to teach you a lesson, that's all.'

'You'd do well to acknowledge before we go any further

with our agreement that I don't take very kindly to being taught lessons. I left the school room a long time ago.'

'You still have a lot to learn,' she bit out.

'Please enlighten me on the things I've neglected to take on board.'

She hurled him a fiery look as she tore her bread into fragments. 'For a start, I don't like being told what to do as if I have no will of my own.'

'Regrettable as that is, I'm the one who has just lost an expensive yacht. Your determination to keep your brother's whereabouts a secret has backfired on you big time. You have only to reveal his details and I will call off the wedding immediately.'

Maddison stared at the crumbs of bread on her plate, her stomach caving in at the thought of revealing Kyle's current address. Could she do it? Could she save her own skin by letting her brother face the music Demetrius Papasakis was intent on personally conducting?

She lifted her gaze to his, defiance in every feature of her expressive face. 'I will never reveal my brother's whereabouts, even if you try and force it out of me.'

He reached for his glass, his eyes as they speared hers dark and dangerous. 'Don't tempt me, Maddison.'

She lowered her gaze to the starched white tablecloth in front of her, her heart thumping erratically in her chest at his implied threat.

The waiter reappeared at their table with a bottle of French champagne, expertly pouring it into the two glasses before leaving them once more to continue their perusal of the extensive menu.

Demetrius picked up his champagne flute and held it up in a toast. 'Here's to us.' His near black eyes glinted with some indefinable quality that made her stomach tighten another sharp little notch.

She picked up her own glass and chinked it against his. 'Here's to my big fat Greek wedding,' she quipped before drinking deeply.

A flicker of amusement passed over his face as he watched her silently. He hadn't thought he would enjoy her company as much as he had; she had a sharp wit and her flashing sapphire-blue eyes were bright with intelligence. He wondered how far she would go before she cracked under the pressure of keeping her brother's whereabouts secret. He hadn't really thought she'd agree to his proposal; in fact he still expected her to pull the plug at the last minute. It amused him to see her squirm, torn between her loyalty towards Kyle and her own freedom, but business was business and he could hardly overlook one point five million dollars.

And, besides, he had to do something about the fuss the press was making. The constant intrusion into his personal affairs was becoming increasingly tiresome; hardly a day passed without his picture appearing somewhere with the usual scathing paragraph accompanying it. It was starting to affect his business reputation, which was a situation he could no longer tolerate. A temporary marriage was a stroke of genius, he congratulated himself as he took a contemplative sip of his champagne; if nothing else it would be entertaining watching Maddison Jones try to out manoeuvre him at every turn, very entertaining indeed.

Maddison felt restless under the silent scrutiny to which she was being subjected. It was bad enough having every other diner glancing pointedly her way without having to suffer the sardonic gleam in Demetrius's eyes as well.

The waiter came over to take their order and close on his heels was a photographer. Maddison's eyes widened in alarm as Demetrius gave the photographer the go-ahead, her fury towards him knowing no bounds as he sat back in his chair with a self-satisfied smile.

The camera flashed just as she opened her mouth to protest, which made her even more annoyed. She waited until the man had moved to the next table before she spoke.

'I suppose you think that was funny?' Her eyes flashed with venomous wrath.

'What's wrong? Don't you like having your picture taken?' He took another leisurely sip of his champagne.

'Not under these sorts of circumstances,' she hissed. 'Besides, I had my mouth open; I'll look like an idiot.'

The corner of his mouth lifted in amusement. 'Then perhaps you should learn to keep your very pretty mouth shut,' he advised.

She took another piece of bread and stuffed it in her mouth to stop herself from giving him the dressing down she felt bubbling up in her throat.

'Come now, Maddison,' he chided her gently when she'd gnawed her way through another two pieces. 'Don't pout; you're supposed to be madly in love with me, remember? This is our first official date; try to look as if you're enjoying it.'

She pushed the rest of the bread away and glared at him. 'How am I supposed to enjoy an evening in your company? You're the most obnoxious man I've ever had the misfortune to meet.'

'You never know, I might greatly improve on acquaintance.'

'I doubt it.'

'Never say never; it's like tempting fate.'

She gave him a caustic look from beneath her lashes. 'You'd have to have a complete personality bypass for me to even consider changing my opinion of you.'

He laughed as he picked up his champagne glass once more, twirling the stem with his long fingers as he watched her struggle to hold on to her temper.

'Let's wait and see, shall we?' He raised his glass to her and, tipping back his head, tossed the contents down his throat.

Maddison watched the up and down movement of his neck as he swallowed the liquid, her pulse suddenly feeling heavy in her veins.

She tore her eyes away and stared at the food the waiter was placing before her, wondering if she'd be able to get a single mouthful past the tight restriction in her throat. She felt as if she'd just stepped into water too deep and dangerous for her, the prospect of escape disappearing like a lifeline carried out of reach with the tide.

She felt sure Demetrius was laughing at her behind the cool façade of his too handsome face. She could see it in his eyes as they rested on her, and the way his mouth lifted up at one corner as his gaze travelled over her lazily, making her skin tighten all over with acute awareness. She didn't want to react to him at all, but somehow whenever that brown-black gaze meshed with hers she felt as if her temperature were increasing, her heart-rate elevating and her legs weakening uncontrollably.

She picked up her fork and tasted the delicious seafood pasta dish, sneaking a covert glance his way.

'Would you like to taste some of mine?' He offered her a small morsel on the tip of his fork, passing it across the table to just in front of her mouth.

With the slightest hesitation she opened her mouth over his fork and took the food, her eyes locking with his as she chewed and swallowed.

'Good?'

She nodded and picked up a forkful of her own dish, leaning across as he had done for him to taste it. His eyes burned into hers as his mouth opened over the food, drawing it into his mouth slowly, his tongue coming out to trace over his lips in a single sweep that sent her blood on a riotous passage through her veins.

She bent her head to her plate once more, forcing herself to eat every scrap in an attempt to keep her gaze from shifting in his direction.

She declined coffee and dessert, not because she didn't want them—she did—but she could no longer trust herself to sit opposite him without betraying how much he affected her.

He settled the bill while she fidgeted uncomfortably under the interested stares of the other diners, angry with herself for wanting to score points off him but even more furious with him for rubbing her nose in it the way he had done.

He took her elbow to lead her out to where he'd parked his car just beyond the world-famous sidewalk café, Harry's Café de Wheels. A chorus of appreciative male whistles sent the colour back to her cheeks as she went past, her head high although she knew her composure was cracking around the edges.

Demetrius held the car door open for her and she slipped under his arm, hoping he couldn't see the bright glitter of angry tears in her eyes.

He strode around to his side and once the car had roared into life turned into the traffic.

'I'd like you to come to my office tomorrow,' he said as he took the turn back to the southern suburbs where she lived. 'I have another document for you to sign.'

She gave him a worried glance. 'More documents? But I already signed the ones you sent.'

'I know but this one is different. At the cessation of our marriage I will be paying you a lump sum to compensate you for any inconvenience you might have suffered.'

'I don't want your money.'

'No, I imagine not, now your brother has already helped himself to a considerable portion of it by destroying my yacht.'

She looked down at her hands, which were twisted in her lap. 'You make it sound as if I deliberately encouraged him.'

'Didn't you?' He slanted a quick glance her way.

'No, of course not.'

'But you do blame me for your father's untimely passing, don't you?'

'I'm surprised you even remember him,' she said with considerable bitterness.

'Your father worked for me for a number of years,' he responded evenly. 'I was generally happy with his work but in the last few months he seemed to run off the rails a bit. I took him to task over some funds he seemed reluctant to account for. The rest, as you know, is history.'

'He did nothing wrong. I know that as surely as I'm sitting here.'

'I understand your loyalty but the fact he refused to answer my questions seemed to be an admission of guilt. I had no choice but to let him go.'

'Why didn't you conduct a proper investigation?' she asked, turning in her seat to look at him.

Demetrius shifted his gaze from hers. 'I got my second in command, Jeremy Myalls to do it. He came up with the same verdict as me. Your father was siphoning off money to fund some scheme of his own.'

'I don't believe it. My father was so careful with money, especially since my mother died.'

'How old were you when she died?'

Maddison felt her hands tighten into knots in her lap. 'Ten. Kyle was five.'

'It must have been very hard for you, being so young.'

'I coped.'

She felt his glance but didn't look his way.

'I did what I could to give your father a way out,' he said into the small silence that had fallen. 'I was very sorry to lose him.'

'Not half as much as me.'

Demetrius turned back to the road ahead, his brow furrowing slightly. It was understandable she'd be loyal to her father's memory but it didn't sit well with him that she'd painted him as the grim reaper who'd hastened her father to his grave. Damn it! He'd liked the guy. He'd done all he could—so had Jeremy—to find out the truth but Bill Jones had remained very tightlipped to the end.

He drove the rest of the distance to her apartment in silence, somehow sensing she was close to tears. It made him feel uncomfortable, a state he wasn't used to feeling if he could get away with it.

As soon as Demetrius pulled up in front of her home Maddison got out of the car without waiting for him to open her door. She was halfway up the path when he caught her, swinging her around to face him, the soft glow of the street light reflecting the bright glitter of tears in her blue eyes as she glared up at him.

'Let me go.' She snatched at her arm and turned for the door.

'Maddison.' He caught the back of her tight sweater and she heard something tear as he pulled her back round to face him.

'Now look what you've done!' she cried as she inspected the loose stitching underneath one arm.

'Stop struggling and hear me out, damn it,' he said impatiently.

'I don't want to talk to you.'

'I don't want you to talk, I want you to listen.'

'I don't want to listen either,' she flared back at him. 'I hate you.'

He held her mutinous look for a tense throbbing moment.

'Then maybe I should give you one more good reason to hate me.' His eyes glittered dangerously as he hauled her closer.

'I couldn't possibly hate you more than I do at this moment,' she bit out furiously.

'Let's see about that, shall we?' he said before he closed the distance between them to crush her mouth beneath the hard insistent pressure of his.

Maddison felt all the fight go out of her with that first kiss. Her body was jammed so tightly up against his she could barely breathe, and her heart was hammering like a wild thing as he deepened the kiss with a bold thrust of his tongue between her softly parted lips. The grazing stroke of his tongue along hers sent fire through her blood, a raging fire that was fast getting out of control. She felt its heat trickle through her, a molten pool settling between her thighs as he pressed her even closer to where the heated trajectory of his arousal pulsed against her unashamedly.

She felt the glide of his warm hand come up to shape her breast, the long fingers close over her possessively. Her breath snagged in her throat as the pad of his thumb found her tight nipple, caressing it repeatedly until she was sure she would cry out with the sensations coursing through her. Her legs were threatening to give way, her spine loosening as if liquid had replaced her bones. She felt as if someone had slipped her a drug so potent that she couldn't think for herself, but had to rely on him to lead her through the maze of her spiralling need.

Her tongue unfolded to dance with his in sharp little steps that tugged at her insides creating an aching emptiness deep within her. She pressed herself even closer, glorying in the feel of his swollen length against the yielding softness of her belly.

She felt him walk her backwards out of the glare of the street light, his thighs in step with her quivering ones, felt the cold concrete retaining wall along the length of her spine as his mouth ground against hers with a fevered intensity. She opened her mouth on a gasp as he freed one pert breast, his hot mouth closing over it greedily. She sagged against the wall and would have fallen if he hadn't been holding her. The sensation of his lips and tongue on the engorged nipple sent every rational thought flying out of her brain.

The sound of a car pulling into the driveway and its subsequent arc of lights separated them.

Demetrius stepped away from her, raking a hand through his thick hair, his chest rising and falling with the hectic pace of his breathing.

Maddison straightened her clothes with as much poise as she could, meticulously avoiding his eye as she did so.

'Maddison,' His voice sounded harsh and she heard the rustle of his clothing as he reached out a hand towards her.

'Goodnight, Demetrius.'

She turned and took the steps to the foyer of her apartment block with a speed he could only admire considering the precarious height of her heels.

He stood silently as the door closed softly behind her, his brows meeting in a slight frown as her footsteps faded away.

He turned back to his car, got in and started it with a roar and drove away, but all the way back to his penthouse he could taste her on his tongue and he could still feel her pliant body imprinted along the hard length of his.

CHAPTER FOUR

MADDISON received a summons from Demetrius's secretary the following day requesting her presence at his office at two p.m.

It annoyed her that he hadn't taken the time to call her himself and she seriously considered not turning up, but at the last minute thought better of it. She wasn't prepared to risk incurring his wrath in case yet again it backfired on her.

She still resolutely refused to think about that kiss.

Every time her tongue touched her lips she snapped her teeth together and distracted herself with something else so she didn't have to think about how his lips had crushed hers. She wouldn't allow herself to recall the feel of his hard thighs pressing her backwards, nor would she give in to the temptation of recalling how his long fingers had felt against her breast, or his hot mouth closing over her nipple.

When she arrived at his office tower she was in no better frame of mind.

Demetrius's secretary greeted her with less haughtiness, and even though her gaze swept over Maddison's worn out trainers and faded jeans and yellowed white top she gave no outward indication of her disapproval.

Demetrius, however, frowned as she entered his office after his command to come in. He reached for something on his desk and handed it to her without a word.

'What is it?' She looked at the envelope suspiciously.

'It's the credit card I sent to you a few days ago which, for some reason, you returned. However, judging from current appearances, it looks like it might come in very useful.'

She straightened her spine and ignored his outstretched hand. 'I don't want your filthy money.'

A tiny nerve pulsed at the side of his mouth as he looked

down at her. 'I suggest you take it and use it to buy the sort of clothes you will need to be my wife for the next few months. If you don't I'll have to dress you each morning myself and, believe me, nothing would give me greater pleasure.'

She took the envelope and stuffed it into the pocket of her jeans with a mutinous scowl.

'Sit down, Maddison,' he commanded. 'I have some things to discuss with you.'

She sat down and folded her arms across her chest.

'My lawyer has prepared some documentation for you to look over and sign.' He handed her a sheaf of papers. 'When our marriage is annulled I will pay you a sum but you get nothing else, understood?'

She sent him an arctic look before lowering her eyes to the papers in her hands.

'I suggest you read through those carefully and see my lawyer,' he continued. 'You're under no pressure to sign, of course, but if you refuse I will have no choice but to pursue criminal charges against your brother.'

She didn't trust herself to speak. She sat fuming at his overbearing manner, wishing she could find some way of paying him back for making her feel so wretched.

'I'd also like you to move out of your apartment the day before the wedding,' he said. 'Since we'll be marrying in the Royal Botanic Gardens the next morning I thought it would be more convenient. I've advised the hotel of your impending arrival and organised a removals firm for your belongings. I've also made an appointment for you with the hotel beauty salon therapist just in case you're tempted to do another routine similar to last night. I wouldn't want you to suffer any further embarrassment.'

She looked up at him at that to see him holding the morning's paper, open at the social pages.

She stared at the photograph which had been taken the night before in the restaurant.

It could hardly be described as flattering. Her mouth looked like a fly trap, her eyes like she had a hangover and her cleavage like a blatant invitation to take liberties. Demetrius, however, looked the urbane businessman he was, even though his smile was faintly mocking.

'I'm sure I'll manage to scrub up on the day,' she said through stiff lips.

'You'd better or you'll have me to answer to.'

A firm knock at the door prevented her from flinging him a stinging reply.

'Come in, Jeremy,' Demetrius called, sending Maddison a warning look as the door opened behind her.

She got to her feet as a man of a similar age to Demetrius approached.

'Miss Jones, how nice to meet you at last.' The blond man took her hand and squeezed it damply. 'I knew your father. A good man; we all miss him dreadfully.'

'Thank you,' she murmured, retrieving her hand from his and only just resisting the urge to wipe it dry against her jeans.

'Demetrius has told me the good news.' He flashed a smile that didn't quite make the distance to his pale blue eyes. 'May I offer my heartiest congratulations?'

'Thank you,' she said again, her cheeks growing warmer by the minute.

'Maddison is going shopping, aren't you, darling?' Demetrius smiled down at her. 'We'll excuse you if you want to get on your way. Jeremy and I have some business to discuss.'

Maddison picked up the sheaf of papers and made her way to the door.

'Aren't you forgetting something?'

She turned, looking at him uncertainly for a long moment.

'Come here, darling,' he coaxed. 'I haven't kissed you good-bye.'

She retraced her steps and lifted her face to his, trying to ignore the taunting light in his dark eyes as he bent his head to hers.

His kiss was blatantly sexual, which made her grow hot all over, particularly with his right-hand man looking on.

Somehow she managed to break the embrace without betraying herself. She lifted her hand in a wave that encompassed them both and left the office with a haste she hoped Jeremy Myalls would put down to her urge to shop and not to the desperate need she had to put some much needed distance between Demetrius Papasakis and herself.

After the brief appointment with Demetrius's lawyer was over she wandered aimlessly around the shops, stopping to look at things occasionally, but after half an hour or so gave up. She decided her lack of shopping prowess was no doubt due to her constant shortage of funds in the past, Kyle's history of disruptive behaviour steadily eating into her resources.

She wondered if perhaps Demetrius was right; she had gone to her brother's rescue too often, but on reflection she couldn't see how she could have done any differently. Ever since their mother had died in a car accident she'd more or less taken on the responsibility of caring for Kyle. She knew deep down he appreciated it, even if he never actually came out and said so. She'd even given up her own hopes of a university education so he could take the lion's share of resources their father had faithfully provided.

It worried her to think of how hard their father had worked to keep the family together. They hadn't been exactly poor but neither had there been a surfeit of funds for the sort of luxuries other people took for granted. She thought about Demetrius's comments about her father's unusual behaviour in the few months before he died. It concerned her that she might have overlooked something which would provide the clue to why Demetrius would adopt that view, but for the life of her couldn't recall anything significant in her father's behaviour. Over the years she'd more or less grown used to his quiet presence in the background. Never a man to talk about his feelings; she had been content to let him be while she got on with the challenge of keeping Kyle on the straight and narrow with varying degrees of success.

But perhaps things hadn't been as straightforward as she'd

assumed. Maybe her father had had worries he hadn't told anyone about, worries that in the end had become too much to cope with. Certainly the details of his estate had been somewhat of a shock to both her and Kyle. Their father's lawyer had told them regretfully of outstanding taxes to pay, funeral costs and other overdue debts that needed immediate settlement. Once all those details had been attended to, however, there had been very little left. There had been no long-term investments, no stocks and bonds, and no savings to speak of. Maddison had had to sell her car to pay for one of Kyle's subsequent misdemeanours as the bank had foreclosed on the house, leaving them without capital.

The more she thought about it she couldn't help feeling guilty for not recognising her brother's deep-seated anger towards Demetrius Papasakis earlier. While she knew Demetrius's actions had no doubt contributed to her father's illness and subsequent death, she hadn't gone so far as to articulate as such. Instead, she'd quietly nurtured her own anger, hoping one day to do something to bring about the justice she knew her father deserved. In the meantime her volatile younger brother had taken his own revenge, an action she could hardly blame him for, considering the grief and loss they'd experienced. The only trouble was that she was now the one paying the price for her brother's impulsive actions and from what she'd seen so far of Demetrius he expected her to pay up in full.

Another day passed without any contact from him and by the end of that evening Maddison started to relax enough to let her breath out in more generous portions. She'd felt on edge all day, waiting for his call or summons, busily rehearsing a hundred excuses to decline whatever date he had organised so he wouldn't be able to call all the shots. But when it got to midnight and he hadn't called at all she became angry. She felt as if he were playing with her, dangling her on the end of his line to draw out her punishment.

Two more days passed and she began to feel the pressure of

the approaching wedding. Demetrius's secretary informed her of the arrangements made on her behalf and Maddison's anger grew steadily.

The removals firm arrived the next morning and she stood by as they set to the task of packing all her things ready to be transported to Demetrius's penthouse or into storage. She opted to take very little with her, preferring to communicate the very temporary nature of their arrangement by keeping her baggage necessarily light.

Once the removal people had finished, she cleaned the apartment before taking the keys to the agent, feeling all the time as if she was stepping into the unknown.

How would she live with a man she hardly knew for an unspecified length of time? Could she trust him to keep the arrangement on paper? She kept reassuring herself he was already involved with Elena Tsoulis and would have no need of her to entertain him, but something in his manner towards her set her on edge. She had never been so acutely aware of a man in her entire life. How could she keep her reactions to him under wraps until the time lapsed? And when he had no further need of her would she be able to walk away without a single backward glance?

Later that day Maddison caught a cab to the Papasakis Park View Tower Hotel and approached the front desk to claim a key as directed by Demetrius's secretary.

'Miss Jones.' The manager on duty smiled at her with warmth. 'Welcome to the Papasakis Park View Tower. I hope your stay with us will be extremely happy.'

'Thank you,' she answered politely.

'Here is your key.' He handed her the key card. 'And if there's anything you require please feel free to call reception at any time. I believe your things have already been delivered. Would you like one of the domestic staff to help you unpack?'

'No, that won't be necessary,' she reassured him. 'Is…is Mr Papasakis upstairs?'

'I believe he is.' The manager smiled. 'Would you like me to call him to tell him you're here?'

'No, I think I'll surprise him myself.' She schooled her features into what she hoped looked like artful playfulness. 'He just loves surprises.'

She swung away towards the lifts with a secret smile; Demetrius Papasakis was in for the surprise of his life, she determined. She wasn't going to meekly fit into his plans as if she didn't have a bone in her back.

She opened the door of the penthouse without hesitation and closed it heavily behind her.

'Hey babe, is that you?' Demetrius's voice called from one of the rooms down the hall.

His endearment threw her somewhat but she rallied valiantly. 'Yes, Cupcake, it's me.'

She heard his heavy strides as he came down the hall and straightened her spine when he came into view. He was wearing gym gear, the white T-shirt sticking to his chest where perspiration had gathered. His long tanned legs seemed to go on for ever, their hard musculature a heady reminder to her of his implacable strength.

His dark eyes swept over her briefly, coming back to settle on her blue eyes.

'Cupcake?' He frowned.

She gave him a guileless look. 'Would you prefer something else?' She put her bag down and kicked off her shoes. 'Sweetie or baby or something?'

'Demetrius will be fine,' he said, watching as she released her hair from its casual ponytail to shake the ash-blonde tresses free.

'God, I'm starving.' She cracked her knuckles in front of her. 'Does this place have room service?'

His eyes narrowed slightly as he looked down at her. 'Just dial nine.'

She brushed past him to look around the penthouse, stopping in front of the huge windows to peer down at the street below.

'Wow, what a view!' She turned back to face him. 'I think I'm going to enjoy living here.'

'I'm very glad to hear it.' His tone suggested anything but, and she smiled another secret inward smile.

'Did you manage to find a suitable wedding dress?' he asked.

'I did, actually.' She plopped down on the nearest leather sofa and put her feet on the coffee table, one of her big toes peeking out from a hole in her sock. 'I made it myself.'

He disguised his grimace well, she thought.

'You didn't need to put yourself to so much trouble,' he said dryly. 'I gave you a credit card.'

'Oh, it was no trouble,' she assured him gaily. 'I had some material left over from the curtains.'

'Curtains?'

'What's wrong?' She gave him a wide-eyed innocent look. 'I paid a lot of money for those curtains, I'll have you know.'

'I don't believe this.' He shook his head as if trying to re-move some sort of gremlin from his brain.

'I thought you'd be pleased.' She gave her version of a pout. 'I didn't see the point in wasting even more money, especially since you've already lost one point five million dollars with your boat.'

'Don't remind me.'

She swung her legs off the coffee table to stand up and stretch, instantly noting the way his dark eyes followed the upward movement of her T-shirt to reveal her toned stomach.

'Have you had dinner?' she asked.

'Not as yet.'

'Shall I order room service for you as well?'

'No, I'm going out.'

'Oh, silly me.' She gave a vacuous giggle. 'It's your buck's night, isn't it?'

'No, actually I was going to see Elena.' He found himself lying for the heck of it. 'I thought that was her when you arrived.'

'Is she coming to the wedding?' she asked, refusing to acknowledge the way his reference to Elena hurt.

'No, I didn't think it appropriate under the circumstances.'

'I guess not,' she said. 'Exactly who is coming?'

'No one you'd know. What about you? Did you get around to inviting anyone?'

'No. I didn't see the point.'

Demetrius's hooded expression gave little away but Maddison knew she had annoyed him. She could sense it in the narrow eyed looks he was sending her way as if he couldn't quite make her out.

'I'm going to have a shower,' he said. 'I'll leave you to make yourself at home.'

'I feel right at home already.' She smiled as she reached for the telephone to dial room service.

'So I see,' he said and turned away.

Maddison smiled to herself as she tucked her feet under her on the sofa; Demetrius Papasakis wasn't going to have things all his own way if she had anything to do with it.

He left a short while later dressed in a casual shirt and trousers, the citrus fragrance of his aftershave lingering in the air long after he'd gone.

She picked at the food she'd ordered with little appetite. She hated to admit it but it annoyed her that he'd gone to be with his mistress the night before his marriage to her. She knew it was silly of her, especially since he'd made it clear the marriage was to be nothing but a charade, but still she felt irritated by his dismissal. She wondered if he was doing it deliberately to remind her of her temporary place in his life, that she had no hold over him at all.

She wandered about the plush penthouse distractedly, wondering if this time she'd bitten off far more than she could chew comfortably. Her little game was likely to backfire on her, for even though he played his cards close to his chest she sensed a brooding, simmering anger just under the surface of the thin veneer of politeness he'd demonstrated earlier.

She waited until as long as she dared for him to return but it was well past midnight when she conceded defeat and curled up in a tight ball in the spare bedroom, her things in various cartons about the room still unpacked. She was increasingly aware of the minutes ticking by, each one drawing her closer to the morning of her marriage to Demetrius.

She heard him come in at about two a.m.

She seriously considered turning off the small bedside lamp but years of habit forestalled her. She hadn't slept without a small light on for years.

She strained her ears, her breath tight in her chest as she listened for any sound of him coming towards her room, but apart from the slight hiss of a tap and the soft clunk of a door closing there was nothing to suggest he had any other intention than going straight to his own bed.

She flung herself on to her stomach in an effort to stop herself thinking about his very male torso lying stretched out in the big bed in the main bedroom, his long, tanned limbs entangled in the sheets, his broad chest rising and falling, his hair tousled, his straight dark brows softened in relaxation and the firm lines of his mouth softening as he gradually drifted off to sleep.

She thumped the pillow and turned over to her back and stared at the lamplight shadows dancing on the ceiling, her hands clenched into fists at her sides.

Damn him! She didn't want to think about him. She didn't want to remember how it felt to have his mouth on hers. Didn't want to imagine what it would feel like to have his hard male body press hers to the mattress, his swollen maleness reaching for her to take her on a journey to paradise. She didn't want to be reduced to a quivering mess of need.

She *mustn't* be reduced to that!

Somehow she must have slept for when she opened her eyes it was fully light and she could hear the sound of him moving about in the penthouse.

She brushed the hair out of her face and, dragging on the

tracksuit she'd worn the day before, came out of the spare room with a casual indifference which she hoped he wouldn't see was entirely forced.

'Good morning.' She padded into the kitchen cheerily.

Demetrius turned at the sound of her voice, his dark eyes running over her briefly before returning to her bed-tousled features. She had a little girl look about her, her shoulder-length hair all awry and her cheeks still slightly flushed from sleep. She looked as if she'd slept in her clothes and he felt a sudden stab of desire deep in his groin when he thought about what she would look like without the armour of unfashionable attire she insisted on wearing in his presence.

'Good morning.' He reached for the coffee pot. 'How did you sleep?'

'You know how it is, the first night in a strange bed.' She stretched her arms above her head and gave a huge yawn.

'Just how many strange beds have you slept in?' he asked, handing her a cup of coffee.

She peeped at him from beneath her lashes as she took the steaming cup. 'I make it a habit to never discuss previous lovers.' She took a tentative sip. 'It's not fair to compare.'

The corner of his mouth lifted slightly as he stood watching her for a long moment. 'That's highly commendable of you. I'm not used to such considerate behaviour in the women I associate with.'

'Perhaps you need to raise the standard of the women you associate with,' she returned.

He gave her another studied look. 'Perhaps I should.'

Maddison found it increasingly difficult to keep her mask of indifference in place under his tightening scrutiny. She felt as if he were peering below the surface of her skin, seeing her for who she really was instead of the caricature she was presenting to him. She needed to remain unaffected by him; it would keep him at arm's length where he belonged.

Just when she thought she could stand his scrutiny no more he turned away to pour some cereal into a bowl.

'I'll be leaving shortly,' he announced without turning around. 'I thought you'd like some privacy to get ready.'

'I'm surprised you trust me to turn up on time,' she couldn't resist saying.

He turned back to face her. 'I've already allowed for the possibility you might do a runner. I've arranged for the beauty therapist to come up here to you and once she is done Jeremy Myalls will accompany you to the Botanic Gardens.'

'I could've arranged for one of my own friends to give me away.'

'You told me you hadn't invited any.'

'I didn't want to embarrass them by inviting them to a meaningless marriage ceremony,' she sniped at him irritably.

'It might appear to be meaningless to you, but let me assure you it means everything to your brother's continued freedom. Just remember that if during the course of the next few hours you are tempted to renege on our deal.'

'I wouldn't dream of it. I'm looking forward to making you regret blackmailing me into marrying you.'

'If you have any plans to embarrass me this morning at the ceremony I'd think again. Firstly, I'm not easily embarrassed and, secondly, you'd be very wise to do as you're told in case things blow up in your face. I wouldn't like to think of your brother suffering undue shame as a result of a petulant prank on your part to gain the upper hand.'

She didn't have an answer at the ready and silently fumed as he ate his cereal without once looking her way.

Once he was finished he left the room and a few minutes later she heard him leave the penthouse, still without another word addressed to her.

Not long after she'd showered there was a discreet knock at the door and she opened it to find a young woman carrying an array of hair and beauty equipment in her arms.

'Miss Jones?' The young woman smiled at her. 'My name is Candice. Mr Papasakis arranged for me to do your hair and make-up.'

'Please come in.' Maddison opened the door wider and forced a smile to her lips.

'Mind you—' Candice gave her another warm smile '—I don't know why he thought it necessary; you look so naturally beautiful already.'

Maddison had never considered her features to be anything out of the ordinary and couldn't help feeling a little touched by the compliment.

She led the way through to the bedroom where her dress was laid out on the bed.

'What a stunning dress!' Candice ran her fingers over the ivory silk reverently. 'Who is the designer?'

It was impossible not to be pleased with the young woman's assumption that her dress had been crafted by an expert hand.

'I made it myself.'

'No kidding?' Candice stared at her in amazement. 'Gosh, I can't even sew on a button without drawing blood.'

'It's not as difficult as it looks,' Maddison said. 'It's such a simple straight up and down design.'

'Which will look absolutely gorgeous on your slim figure.' Candice shot an envious glance at the flat plane of Maddison's stomach before returning to her face. 'Are you wearing a veil?'

She shook her head. 'I didn't think it necessary.'

'Maybe you're right,' Candice mused as she opened and un-coiled her hair-dryer. 'Better to let your husband see what he's getting, eh?'

'Yes, something like that,' she answered dryly.

Within a short space of time Candice had arranged Maddison's hair in a casual but elegant knot on top of her head with a few tendrils strategically loosened to fall softly over one eye. She then went on to apply a light covering of make-up to highlight the sapphire blue of her eyes and a soft rose lip-gloss to draw attention to the curve of her mouth. Her dark lashes were lengthened with mascara and her cheeks defined with a subtle blush.

Candice stood back and gave a smile of approval. 'You look fabulous. That handsome husband to be of yours is going to have his socks knocked off when he sees you coming towards him.'

Maddison stood up and twirled in front of the mirror, somewhat pleased to see the dress she'd made so hurriedly cling lovingly to her slim curves, flowing about her ankles like a soft cloud.

She wasn't so sure about Demetrius's reaction, however. He had eyes for no one else but Elena Tsoulis and it would do her a power of good to keep reminding herself of the fact. This was a paper marriage, a hands-off arrangement to keep the baying hounds of the press off his back. She had no right to think of him in any way other than as the man who'd been instrumental in bringing about her father's fatal collapse, and as the man who stood between her younger brother and freedom. She had to maintain her hatred of him at all costs. He was the enemy and she mustn't forget it.

He was the enemy.

CHAPTER FIVE

JEREMY MYALLS arrived not long after Candice had left. Maddison found his sweeping all encompassing gaze a trifle unsettling as it ran over her.

'You look rather delectable.' He took her hand in his and held it for a fraction too long. 'Lucky Demetrius.'

'Shall we go?' she said, scooping up the single creamy rose the florist from downstairs had sent up prior to Jeremy's arrival.

They went downstairs to where a white Mercedes was waiting. Maddison smiled shyly at the hotel staff on the way past the front reception and slipped into the plush interior of the car, wondering if every bride felt the same trapped bird flutters of panic in her stomach as she travelled towards the destination of her wedding ceremony.

The fresh spring air did a lot to settle her nerves once they arrived at the Royal Botanic Gardens. A light breeze coming off the harbour lifted her hair and gave some much needed colour to her cheeks as she walked with Jeremy towards a small knot of people standing overlooking Farm Cove.

Her eyes went immediately to the tallest amongst them. Demetrius was in a charcoal suit with a white shirt and silk tie looking every inch the proud groom. Her eyes clashed with his as she drew nearer, seeing the gleam of satisfaction reflected there as if he were congratulating himself on bringing about his particular form of revenge.

She gritted her teeth behind her small smile and took his hand as the celebrant drew the small crowd together to start the proceedings.

Maddison tried not to listen to the solemn words too much. She hated thinking about the false promises she was making, nor did she wish to think about the way she was tying herself, albeit temporarily, to such a ruthless man as Demetrius Papasakis. She kept reminding herself she was doing it to protect her brother, but as Demetrius slipped the gold band on to her finger she felt a shiver of something unrecognisable go through her as if something elemental had just passed between them in that simple act.

She vaguely registered the celebrant's words for him to kiss the bride and her eyes fluttered closed as his head came lower, his breath caressing her up-tilted face before his firm mouth came down to press against hers. She felt the soft stroke of his tongue, its movement in her mouth holding a sensual promise she found hard to ignore. She kept reminding herself he was doing it for the crowd's sake, but her own response had nothing whatsoever to do with the people watching and she wondered if he knew it.

'I now present to you all, Mr and Mrs Demetrius Papasakis,' the celebrant announced proudly as Demetrius broke the kiss.

The small crowd went wild with applause and Maddison found herself caught up in their enthusiasm, even smiling widely as several paparazzi cameras flashed in her face.

'You look beautiful.' Demetrius lowered his head to speak to her, his warm breath curling around her ear.

'Did I have you worried?' she asked with a spark of spirit in her eyes as she looked up at him.

His gaze slipped to where the neck of her dress hinted at the soft curves of her breasts, lingering there for a moment before returning to her face.

'That dress would be wasted covering a window.' He smiled a lazy half-smile. 'And I'm beginning to think it's a terrible waste covering your body as well.'

She wasn't sure how to answer him. A part of her wished she had the sophistication to laugh off his flirtatious comment, recognising it as the sort of thing men say to women all the time, but another perverse little part of her wished he'd meant it sincerely.

'Come.' He took her arm in his and led her to where the

photographer was waiting. 'We have some official photographs to do before the champagne begins to flow.'

Maddison walked alongside him, very conscious of the hard length of his thigh against hers as he held her close.

She forced a smile to her lips as the photographer clicked his way through a series of shots, doing her best to look the part of the ecstatic bride while inside she was feeling increasingly apprehensive. Demetrius in this lightly flirting mood was a danger to her carefully constructed defences and she knew she'd have to keep her wits about her to avoid being drawn even further into his orbit of charm.

Once the photographer was finished with the official photographs Demetrius led the way back to where the cars were waiting outside the Opera House. Maddison walked by his side with her hand in the warm, firm grasp of his, her heart beating an erratic tattoo in her chest as she thought about what she'd just done.

She was married to him, committed in a way she hadn't thought possible less than ten days ago.

She wondered what he was thinking as he handed her into the waiting car. Was he secretly gloating about his victory in bringing herself and Kyle to heel? Or was he busily planning his next clandestine assignation with his lover?

The reception was held in one of plush rooms of the Papasakis Park View Tower Hotel, and it was clear as soon as they entered the beautifully decorated room that no expense had been spared to ensure the occasion would be remembered as nothing short of lavish.

Demetrius handed her a glass of champagne as the waiter passed, clinking his own glass against hers, his dark eyes mysterious as they meshed with hers.

'To a productive union,' he said.

The sound of his glass against hers seemed to her to be exaggeratedly loud as if all the other background noise in the room had faded into insignificance.

She drank from her glass, all the time avoiding his eyes,

desperate to conceal from him her increasing vulnerability to him.

Jeremy Myalls approached with an almost finished measure of Scotch in his hand and a smile on his lips that wasn't reflected in his cold washed-out blue gaze.

'My congratulations to you both,' he said, his eyes lingering on Maddison's cleavage, before turning to Demetrius. 'Are you planning on going on a honeymoon?'

'No—'

'Of course,' Demetrius cut off her denial. 'We'll be leaving after the reception. I've left details of how I can be contacted with my secretary if anything should come up that needs my urgent attention.'

Maddison was almost certain that Jeremy looked a little put out that he hadn't been informed previously of his boss's arrangements. She felt a little irritated as well. How dare he take her on a honeymoon without discussing it first with her?

She waited until Jeremy had moved away to speak to another guest before confronting Demetrius.

'I'm not sure how I'm supposed to get through a honeymoon without sufficient notice. I don't have anything packed,' she said in a tight undertone. 'Anyway, I thought once today was over it was business as usual.'

'It is business as usual,' he replied smoothly, his eyes coming to rest on Jeremy Myalls, who was across the room.

'But I don't want to go on a honeymoon with you.'

After a moment he looked down at her as if he didn't know how she'd come to be standing by his side. 'Will you excuse me?' He frowned. 'I have something to see to.'

She didn't get the chance to respond for he'd already moved away, leaving her with a half empty champagne glass and a sinking feeling in the pit of her stomach.

She turned away and smiled at one of the guests as they approached.

'Hello, Maddison,' an older woman said, taking her hand in hers. 'I'm Nessa Koulos. I've wanted to meet you ever since Demetrius told me he'd found the woman of his dreams.'

Maddison couldn't imagine Demetrius speaking of her in such a way; it was more likely he'd describe her as the woman of his worst nightmare if the truth were to be told.

'I'm very pleased to meet you,' she said, shaking the other woman's hand, hoping her surprise wasn't showing. 'Have you known Demetrius long?'

'It seems for ever.' Nessa gave a self-effacing grin. 'But then we more or less grew up together. We're cousins, you see.'

'Oh, I didn't know...'

'Demetrius doesn't talk much about his family,' Nessa went on. 'His parents' divorce hit him hard, he was so young. My parents and I were his second family during the worst of it.'

Maddison wasn't sure how to respond. She didn't want Demetrius's cousin to think she knew nothing of her new husband's background but she was torn with the desire to find out more about the things that had shaped his character.

'We haven't had much time to talk about our respective families,' she said carefully.

Nessa gave an amused laugh. 'Yes, it was rather a whirlwind courtship, wasn't it? But then, your father worked for him for years, isn't that so?'

'Yes,' Maddison answered without elaborating any further.

'You have a younger brother, don't you?' Nessa asked, scooping up a glass of champagne from a passing waiter.

'Yes, he's...working interstate at present.'

'Oh? Where?' She took a sip of the bubbling liquid, her dark eyes on Maddison's face.

Maddison wasn't so foolish as to fall into such a carefully laid trap. She had no idea if Demetrius had organised for his cousin to milk her for information about Kyle's whereabouts and she wasn't going to take the risk no matter how nice Nessa appeared to be.

'I'm not exactly sure where he is right at this point,' she answered with the bare minimum of truth she could comfortably get away with. 'He moves about a bit. You know what young men are like.'

'I do,' Nessa agreed wryly. 'I have two boys of my own,

nineteen and twenty-one. Never a dull moment, I can assure you.'

Maddison sipped at her own champagne, hoping the conversation would soon shift to another topic.

'I'm so glad Demetrius has come to his senses and settled down,' Nessa said after a pause. 'He's been playing the field too long. It's high time he sired a son or two to carry on the family name.'

'We haven't discussed children as yet,' Maddison said, hoping her cheeks weren't as hot as she felt inside.

'Don't leave it too long,' Nessa said. 'Demetrius is almost thirty-five; he needs a solid base to come home to. A happy home would do wonders for him.'

'I'll do my best.' Maddison avoided the other woman's eye.

'I know you've probably heard all about his relationship with Elena Tsoulis,' Nessa said after a small pause. 'I wouldn't worry about it if I were you. Elena knows which side her bread is buttered; her ex-husband, Mikolas, is watching her every move. I'm sure she's only been playing with Demetrius to get Mikolas's attention; she should never have divorced him in the first place. Greek men can be very territorial about their women, as I'm sure you've heard.'

'Yes, I had heard something to that effect.'

'Don't look so frightened.' Nessa smiled reassuringly. 'I'm sure Demetrius won't be too hard on you.'

'I'll have to do my very best to behave.'

'How terribly boring, my dear,' Nessa said. 'You keep him guessing for as long as you can; men like Demetrius just love a challenge.'

'Yes, I have noticed.'

'Underneath that high-powered exterior a real man's heart is beating,' Nessa added. 'Don't lose sight of that no matter what happens.'

Maddison was almost relieved when someone attracted Nessa's attention and she excused herself to go over to speak with them. The reprieve gave her time to absorb Demetrius's cousin's revelations, which had shown a side of him previously unknown to her. She wondered about his family background, how his parents' divorce had affected him. Nessa hadn't indicated his exact age at the time but somehow she assumed he hadn't been all that old. She also wondered if either of his parents was still alive and whether he had any contact with them. She backtracked over the various conversations they'd had but couldn't recall a single mention of anything to do with his family. It seemed strange now she'd had time to reflect on it. Maybe Nessa was right, there was more to Demetrius than met the eye; the only trouble was, did she want to see what it was?

Demetrius came back to her side to farewell the departing guests prior to their own departure. Maddison stood by his side, his arm around her waist, smiling at the various friends and associates as if she couldn't be happier, when in fact she wished no one was leaving yet so that she would have a little more time to prepare herself for whatever he had planned in terms of a honeymoon. It still annoyed her that he hadn't mentioned his intention of carrying the charade of their marriage that far. It made her feel as if she were acting in a play without seeing the script first.

The last of the guests had left when he turned to her, dropping his arm from about her waist.

'I'll meet you upstairs shortly,' he said. 'Pack a few things for a weekend in the country. I won't be long.'

She watched as he disappeared through the double doors of the reception room, her brow furrowing at his curt dismissal.

She turned on her heel and, giving the waiting staff a defiant look, picked up a fresh glass of champagne from the nearest table and took it with her towards the lifts.

She stabbed at the call button and while she waited sipped agitatedly at her drink, anger curling like a serpent in her belly. She wondered if he'd slipped out for a quick liaison with Elena before returning to act out the role of besotted husband.

When the lift arrived she decided on impulse to get off on the fifth floor where a cocktail bar was situated. If Demetrius was going to think she would be ready and waiting when he returned he could think again.

The young cocktail host came over with the drinks menu and an appreciative male smile.

'Good evening, Mrs Papasakis, what can I get you to drink?'

Maddison hadn't expected to be recognised and wondered if it had been wise to try to get the upper hand when the playing field was now so unbalanced. She wondered if Demetrius had sent out a brief on her, informing his staff of her arrival at the hotel.

She gave an answering smile and after the briefest glance at the menu chose the first item that caught her eye.

'I'll have a Mai Tai, thank you.'

'Won't be a moment,' he said and bowed away.

Maddison sat somewhat self-consciously as he went away to fetch her drink. She wasn't all that comfortable in bars at the best of times; to be sitting in one owned by the man who was now her husband made it even more unusual. But he wasn't just her husband, she reminded herself, he was the man responsible for her brother's exile and her father's early death. She had to keep that at the forefront of her mind at all times, especially now as his ruthless machinations had brought about their marriage.

For that alone she hated him with a passion. She was nothing more than a toy he'd decided to play with for a short while. He'd used her vulnerability over Kyle's behaviour to achieve his own ends. She wasn't all that sure she believed his story about needing a cover-up relationship; it didn't make sense that he would need to go to such lengths. He was unbelievably wealthy and used to taking control. It seemed unthinkable that he would allow himself to bow to public pressure in such a way. He was a man who was quite clearly used to getting his own way no matter who or what obstructed him. With a click of those long masculine fingers he could remove any obstacles without a single flicker of conscience if indeed he even had one.

The more she thought about it the more she began to recognise the devious way his mind worked. He was obviously using her as an insurance policy to make her pay for the loss of his boat, knowing she would never reveal her brother's whereabouts to him even under threat. And he'd certainly threatened her. She still got the shivers when she thought about that kiss.

Her drink arrived and she took a tentative sip before setting it down again.

Several people had drifted into the bar and before she could shrink back to avoid being noticed a blond head turned in her direction and a cold blue gaze singled her out.

She had no choice but to acknowledge Jeremy Myalls as he sauntered over, a drink in his hand and a smile lifting one edge of his mouth as his eyes ran over her.

'Don't tell me Demetrius has deserted you already?'

'Not at all.' She reached for her cocktail. 'I'm just about to go upstairs to pack for our honeymoon.'

She hoped she was giving a convincing picture of the happy bride anticipating her first night of marriage but somehow something in Jeremy's expression informed her she hadn't been all that successful.

'I would've thought that a superfluous task,' he commented lazily. 'The last thing one needs on one's honeymoon is clothes.'

She felt her cheeks grow warm as a vision of Demetrius without clothing flitted into her mind. She could almost see the ripple of toned muscles, the long hard flanks of his thighs and what lay potently between them...

She tossed back the rest of her drink and got to her feet with a wavering smile. 'I'd better be going. Have a nice evening, Mr Myalls.'

'Jeremy,' he insisted, touching her arm for a second or two longer than necessary.

'Jeremy,' she repeated.

'Have a great honeymoon,' he added as she went past.

'Thank you.'

She got to the lifts and stabbed at the call button. The doors sprang open and she pressed the button for the penthouse floor, leaning back against the mirrored panels as a sweeping tiredness overcame her. A combination of emotional distress and an unfamiliar amount of alcohol had finally taken its toll. All she wanted to do was find a quiet room and fall into a dreamless sleep.

The lift opened with a soft mechanical hiss and she stepped out. She reached for her key card but before she could swipe it the door of the penthouse opened and Demetrius stood there, his dark eyes noting the suddenly guilty look in her blue gaze.

'What took you so long? Did you take the stairs?'

'The lift was slow.' She avoided his eyes. 'It stopped at every floor.' She brushed past him to enter the penthouse but before she could get by he reached out a hand and stalled her, swinging her around to face him.

'Something you'd do very well to take note of before this marriage is much older is that I won't tolerate being lied to. Is that clear?'

She lifted her chin to meet his dark gaze. 'There's something you need to take note of as well; I won't be manhandled by you whenever you feel like it.' She wrenched her arm from his grasp and glared up at him.

'Who were you with just then?' he growled at her.

She took offence at his proprietorial manner even while part of her insisted she tell him what had taken place in the bar with Jeremy Myalls. Her concerns about Kyle, however, overruled her conscience; she owed Demetrius nothing, she reminded herself. He'd blackmailed her into this arrangement and she didn't have to answer to him about her movements.

'Wouldn't you like to know?' she taunted. 'I could, of course, ask you the very same question.'

'But you already know the answer, don't you, Maddison?'

She did and it sickened her to be reminded of it. 'I have no interest in your affair with Elena Tsoulis. It's nothing to me.'

'Not the least bit jealous?'

'Why should I be jealous?' She met his dark satirical gaze

with defiance. 'I don't care what you do with other women as long as you don't expect me to join the throng.'

'Are you worried I might insist on my conjugal rights?'

'Not the least bit worried,' she lied.

'You trust me that far?'

'No,' she said. 'I don't trust you at all, but I can assure you if you try to coerce me I'm sure I'll have the willpower to withstand any of your paltry attempts to seduce me.'

'Paltry attempts?' He tasted the words as a smile played at his lips. 'Is that your assessment thus far?'

She gave him a fulminating look. 'You'll have to try much harder, Demetrius Papasakis, if you want me to capitulate to your particular version of charm. I like my men honest and up front, not conniving and calculating.'

'Conniving and calculating am I now? What a deplorable opinion you have of me. I see I shall have to work extra hard to change your mind then.'

'Even if you sprouted wings and a halo I wouldn't be all that impressed.'

He gave a soft laugh as he looked down at her infuriated features.

'No, I can see it's going to take a whole lot more to convince you I'm not quite the devil you think I am. But we have a few months, so who knows what will happen between now and then?'

'I can make a fair guess. I'm going to hate you even more than I do now.'

'Those are fighting words.' He touched a long finger down the curve of her cheek as his eyes burned into hers. 'And I for one just love a fight.'

Maddison opened her mouth to speak but before the words could come out his head came down and his firm mouth covered hers.

As much as she fought against it she felt desire tug at her insides as his tongue unfolded inside her mouth, drawing from her the sort of response she'd had no intention of giving. She felt as if he had taken control of her will, turning her to mouldable putty in his hands as soon as he touched her. His lips were warm and coercive, his tongue commanding and alluring as it duelled with hers in a battle to conquer. She was losing ground fast, her legs softening beneath her until she was sure she was going to slip to a pool of feeling at his feet. His arms tightened around her, drawing her closer. She felt the hard thrust of his aroused length against her, its implacable presence a reminder of his superior strength and her capitulating weakness.

She wanted him.

She wanted him as she had wanted no one before. Her untutored body was clamouring for a release she knew instinctively he would give unreservedly, powerfully, unforgettably.

He pressed her back against the wall as he continued his assault on her senses. His teeth took her bottom lip in a grazing hold, only to release it for his tongue to salve its swollen surface in a sensuous glide that sent arrows of hot need to her very core, his body grinding into hers, leaving her in no doubt of his pulsing need.

He lifted his mouth off hers to look down at her, his breathing uneven, his eyes aflame with desire.

'Still hate me?'

She sent her tongue out to her lips before answering. 'As much as ever, if not more so.'

'Good.' His smile was mocking. 'I wouldn't want the war to be over just yet. I have a few more battles to win first.'

'This is all a game to you, isn't it?' she tossed at him crossly. 'A game where only you can win because you keep changing the rules.'

'The rules are the same as arranged.'

'Oh, really?' She gave him a cynical look. 'What about the hands off bit of our arrangement?'

'I won't force you to do anything you're not prepared to do.'

'How absolutely typical! No, you won't force me but you'll make it damn near impossible to resist!'

He quirked a dark brow expressively. 'So you do admit to being tempted?'

'No!' she denied hotly. 'I admit nothing.'

His smile deepened as he watched the colour fire in her cheeks. 'Come now, Maddison; let's not start our honeymoon on the wrong foot. Pack; we'll be leaving in ten minutes.'

'I don't want to go on a honeymoon. I don't want to go anywhere with you.'

'Ten minutes, Maddison or I'll carry you down to the car in what you're wearing.'

His eyes challenged her to defy him and she lost a whole minute trying to win that round.

'Nine minutes,' he said. 'And still counting.'

She swung away on a furious breath and, stalking to the spare bedroom, slammed the door behind her.

Throwing her wedding dress to one side, she dressed in casual clothes before stuffing a few items of clothing in a weekend bag as well as her toiletries from the bathroom, all the while fuming at his overbearing manner, he treated her as if she were a particularly recalcitrant child who needed a firm hand.

She had to learn how to resist him! What was wrong with her? She hated him more than anyone she could think of, so why couldn't she resist his mouth and hands? It didn't make sense.

She'd always imagined desire and love to be inextricably linked, for women at least, if not for men. And Demetrius Papasakis was the worst kind of man with whom to get involved—a wealthy playboy with a sexual history that probably read longer than *War and Peace*.

She had no business feeling attracted to him, especially when he could so easily destroy her brother's future with a single phone call to the police. She had to stop herself from responding to him!

She joined him in the spacious lounge, her features still set in mutinous lines, her anger at him pulsing inside her so heavily it took everything she possessed to contain it.

Anger was good. She had to keep angry at him no matter what.

Demetrius took her bag without a word and she snatched her hand away as his fingers touched hers.

'I've asked for my car to be brought around to the front of the hotel,' he said. 'I hope I don't need to remind you we will be in the presence of other people for a few minutes.'

'I'm surprised you don't carry around a clipboard and scene cutting card,' she threw at him scornfully. 'Just so I don't miss my cue.'

He gave her a hard look as he opened the door. 'Behave yourself, Maddison,' he warned. 'Remember your brother's continued freedom depends on it.'

She followed him to the lift, relieved that no one was in it so she had a little more time to prepare herself. The thought of pretending to be in love with him was anathema to her in her current state of heightened rage. She couldn't help feeling he'd deliberately goaded her to make the task even more difficult for her.

The lift doors opened and she fixed a smile on her face as they made their way to the front doors of the hotel.

'Good evening, Mr and Mrs Papasakis,' the evening duty manager said as they moved past reception.

'Thank you, Eric,' Demetrius responded. 'Have a good one yourself.'

Instead of his usual black Jaguar, a large four-wheel drive vehicle was waiting for him, growling like a predatory animal in the driveway.

Maddison sent him another fake smile as he held her door for her, conscious of the baggage boy loading their things into the car.

'Thank you...*darling*.'

His eyes sent her a warning that caused a flicker of sensation to settle between her thighs. She snapped her knees together as he closed the door, trying not to watch as he strode around to the driver's side but unable to stop herself. He had such a commanding presence, his height and stance so compelling she had to forcibly drag her gaze away to stare at her hands in her lap instead.

The car prowled out of the driveway with a low pitched roar, leaving the city behind within a few short minutes.

'Where are we going?' she asked in a stiff voice.

She felt his sideways glance but didn't turn his way.

'I have a little place in the country,' he informed her. 'At Black Rock Mountain.'

She'd never heard of Black Rock Mountain but she could just imagine his little place; it was no doubt huge, with every mod con and a team of obsequious staff to satisfy his every need.

'Another one of your hotels?' Disdain coloured her tone.

'No, strange as it may seem to you, I don't spend all of my time in my hotels.'

'No, of course not.' She sent him a scathing look. 'You spend a great deal of your time in your many lovers' bedrooms. How silly of me to forget.'

His eyes met hers in the intimate darkness of the car as he stopped at traffic lights.

A strange tension began to build in the stretching silence as the powerful car thrummed beneath his control. She couldn't help thinking that somehow he was communicating something through the way he drove it to warn her about him—the tightly leashed power straining underneath his hands, waiting for the command to let go, with no doubt devastating results for anything or anyone who stood in its way.

Yes, the powerful vehicle was definitely an extension of him and she'd do very well to be mindful of it. He could strike without warning, pounce on her, and consume her totally.

The lights changed and the car surged forward with a screech of tyres, the g force sending her backwards in her seat.

He didn't say a word but his silence spoke a thousand for him.

He overtook six cars at a stretch once they hit the motorway, one hand on the wheel, the other resting idly on the arm rest, his dark features set in stone, his expression unreadable.

Maddison found the experience of sitting beside him unnerving to say the least. The silence was intimidating, and even though she speculated on what he was thinking beneath that implacable mask he was impossible to read, which intensified her disquiet.

She stared out at the dark shapes of trees as they flashed past, the rhythmic motion finally completing the work her earlier cocktail and emotional rollercoaster of a day hadn't quite managed to do. Her eyelids dropped, her shoulders relaxed and her head shifted sideways until it rested against the leather upholstery.

The car came to a stop and she jerked awake. 'Where are we?'

He killed the engine and the sudden encroaching darkness as the headlights snapped off felt instantly menacing.

'We're at my retreat.'

She peered out into the impenetrable darkness of the moonless night. She couldn't see any sign of a plush hotel, nor indeed any sort of high life mansion. All she could make out in the darkness was a small hutlike structure that looked as if it badly needed a coat of paint.

'*This* is it?' She gave him an incredulous look.

He opened the car door and the interior light came on. 'This is it.'

She watched as he unfolded his long length from the car and went around to the back to take something from the boot.

A torch snapped on and in its arc of light she could see the hut more clearly.

It wasn't all that encouraging.

It was hardly the place one would expect to spend a honeymoon, even a pretend one, she decided as she got out of the car.

Demetrius had taken the torch with him to unlock the door of the hut, but privately Maddison wondered why he'd felt the need to lock it in the first place. The thick bush surrounding them acted as a screen for absolute privacy; it was quite clear no one would accidentally stumble upon the place unless they'd been given specific directions.

She stood back as he opened the weathered timber door,

hoping no scurrying critters had taken up residence in his absence.

'Aren't you going to switch the lights on?' she asked once he got inside.

He came back out and shone the torch in her face. 'There are no lights.'

She held up her hand against the glare of the torchlight. 'What do you mean there aren't any lights?'

He shifted the torch beam so she could open her eyes. 'There's no power here.'

'No power?' She gaped at him. '*Hello?* This is the twenty-first century. Everyone this side of Bourke has power!'

'Not this place.'

'Why the hell not?'

He stepped down the timber steps and the torch hit her in the face again.

'Will you stop waving that thing in my face all the time?'

'Sorry.' He snapped it off.

'No!' She clutched at him in the darkness. 'Turn it back on!'

'What's wrong? Don't tell me you're frightened of the dark.'

She was twenty-four years old. How the hell could she admit to anyone, least of all him, that she was absolutely terrified of the dark?

'No, of course not!' She forced herself to step back from him. 'I just don't want to lose my footing on this rough ground.' She was pleased with her explanation; it sounded reasonable enough to be convincing.

'You go inside,' he said. 'I'll bring in the things from the car.'

She stood uncertainly, staring through the inky darkness at the black hole of the door.

'I'll help you.' She swung around to follow him, her feet almost tripping over themselves in her haste.

'Careful,' he warned as he shone the torch across the ground at her feet. 'You don't want to break a leg out here.'

'I should have thought of that earlier,' she muttered under

her breath as she hovered around the edges of his torch beam like a tiny ineffectual moth that had nothing better to do.

'What was that?' The torch hit her in the eyes again.

'Nothing.' She shielded her face.

She heard him gather their belongings and crept closer, trying to stay somewhere within the soft beam of light under his command.

'Here, you take the torch.' He handed it to her. 'I'll take the bags.'

She clutched at the cylindrical tube like a drowning person did a lifeboat.

'Watch out for spiders,' he said as they entered the hut.

She almost dropped the torch as she swung it around to his face. *'Spiders?'*

He pushed her arm down so the light was out of his eyes. 'There's not a single spider in here, I can assure you.'

Relief sent her breath out in a rush. 'Phew!'

'They're all married with large families,' he added with a teasing smile.

Cold fear trickled along her spine. In fact she couldn't help thinking a hundred spiders were making their way up to the back of her neck with tiny feathering steps.

'Oh, my God!'

'You are scared.'

'No!' She denied it with sinking courage. 'I can handle a few harmless spiders.' She disguised her shudder well, she thought, glad of the cloak of darkness for probably the very first time in her life.

'I have matches and candles somewhere.' He began searching along what appeared to be a mantle shelf.

She watched as he lit a spindly candle, the tiny flame highlighting his dark satirical features as he turned to face her.

'Do you have a fireplace?' Hope crept into her tone.

'Sure I do.' He struck another match along the side of the box and bent down to light the set fire in the hearth behind him.

'I love fires,' she said. 'No one has fires any more.'

'Central heating certainly has a lot to answer for,' he agreed.

Maddison couldn't believe the sense of relief she felt as the flames started to dart about and take hold. She had to stop herself moving even closer to hold her hands to its warmth, even though by early spring standards the night wasn't all that cold.

'Keep your eye on that while I get us something to drink,' he said, moving away.

She was nothing short of assiduous in her attempts to keep the fire blazing, piling on wood until the towering pyre threatened to topple over and spill out on to the floor.

'Careful,' Demetrius cautioned as he handed her a glass of wine. 'That's all the wood we have until morning.'

She stared at the leaping flames and wondered if she should take off the piece she'd just balanced on top.

'Don't you have a wood-pile outside?'

'I chop it as I need it. I like the exercise.'

It was certainly a side to him she hadn't expected. Never had she imagined he would step outside his billionaire comfort zone to light his own fires and chop his own wood.

It made her wonder if she had missed something somewhere. She was usually so good at reading people, working out who was genuine, who was not, but somehow he'd slipped past her usually meticulous assessment.

'Is it safe to assume this rustic paradise of yours stretches itself to beds?' she asked.

His eyes met hers across the flickering glow of the fireplace.

'It has one bed,' he said. 'Mine.'

CHAPTER SIX

MADDISON stared at him in alarm.

'I'm not sleeping with you!'

'Then where will you sleep?' he asked. 'Outside?'

Her mouth dropped open in panic. 'You can't be serious! I can't sleep outside—it's dark and cold and—'

'Then you'll have to share my bed.'

'I'd rather take my chances with the wildlife out there!'

'I have it on good authority the life out there is pretty wild,' he said smoothly.

She snapped her teeth together in anger. He was goading her deliberately, she could tell. Surely he didn't expect her to sleep with him?

But…outside?

She gave an inward shudder—scorpions, spiders, centipedes and mosquitoes ruled outside.

She lifted her chin and faced him determinedly. 'I suppose you think this is highly amusing, dragging me to this God-forsaken place to teach me some sort of lesson.'

'What sort of lesson would that be?'

'I don't know,' she said. 'You tell me.'

He took a leisurely sip of his wine.

She examined his handsome face for some clue to what he was up to but he was as inscrutable as ever.

'I can assure you, Maddison, I have no such goal in mind. I simply wanted to get us out of the city, away from prying eyes so we could adjust to our situation.'

'We wouldn't even be in this situation if you hadn't insisted on your pound of flesh.'

'We wouldn't be in this situation if your brother hadn't stuck a diving spear through the bottom of my yacht.'

'Is that how he did it?' she blurted without thinking. How in the world had Kyle got his hands on a diving spear?

He must have seen the question in her eyes.

'Not once, not twice, but three times,' he said. 'He was obviously very determined, which I observe seems to be somewhat of a family trait.'

'I don't know what you're talking about.' She lowered her gaze. 'Kyle can barely swim a length of a pool. How could he possibly be responsible for diving underneath your boat and doing that sort of damage?'

'It's amazing what people will do when suitably motivated.'

'Yes, that is certainly something I've recently observed,' she said wryly.

'Meaning?'

'Meaning: why did you insist on marrying me?'

'You know why.'

'I don't believe you needed to escape the press so badly. You must have some other motive, although it beats me what it might actually be.'

'I told you, you're my insurance policy. I lost my boat but I got you instead.'

'I don't mean to take anything away from myself, but for one point five million dollars don't you think you might have been a little short-changed?'

'That remains to be seen.'

'What do you mean?' She eyeballed him. 'You can't mean to go back on your word?'

'What word was that?'

Her eyes widened in fear. 'You promised this was a hands-off arrangement.'

'Did I?'

'You know you did!'

He took another contemplative sip of wine.

Maddison clenched and unclenched her hands by her sides, agitation in every sharp angle of her slim body.

'This is abduction, you know; you'll go to prison.'

'I don't think so.'

The confidence in his tone totally derailed her. She felt a bubble of hysteria rise in her throat and there was nothing she could do to stop it.

She turned away before he could catch sight of the glitter of tears in her eyes. She stared at the corrugated iron-clad wall in front of her and wondered what nightmare she'd inadvertently wandered into.

She heard the chink of his glass as he set it down and then the sound of him stoking the fire, the up-shaft of sudden warmth reaching her across the room.

She took a deep breath and turned back to face him. 'I need to use the bathroom.'

'Which one?'

She looked at him blankly for a second or two. 'You have two?'

'There is a small shower behind that door there.' He pointed to a shadowed corner of the room. 'And out there behind the wood supply is the toilet.'

Her eyes went out on stalks. *It's outside?*

'You can take the torch,' he offered helpfully.

She let out her breath in a rush and swung away in high agitation. 'I can't believe this! This is a nightmare!'

'This is bush life.' He spoke from behind her. 'I admit it's a little rustic, but I like it.'

She turned back round to glare at him.

'Rustic? It's positively primitive! You can't be seriously expecting me to…to…' She gave the door leading outside a worried glance.

'Where's your sense of adventure?' he chided. 'People pay big money for this sort of alternative experience.'

'I thought people paid big money to stay in plush hotels.'

He gave a shrug of one broad shoulder. 'A change is as good as a holiday.'

'This is not my idea of a holiday,' she spat. 'Nor is it anywhere near what I would expect a honeymoon to be like.'

'You were expecting a proper honeymoon?' His eyes caught and held hers.

'No! Of course not. I just meant…you know…we're supposed to be pretending to…'

'What better way to pretend wedded rapture than total seclusion in the wilderness?' He passed. 'Would you like me to come with you to the toilet?'

'No! I would not!' She snatched up the torch from the small table in the middle of the room and made her way to the door.

'If you're not back in ten minutes I'll come and look for you.'

She didn't answer other than to slam the rickety door behind her.

She stood outside the hut for a moment or two, trying to get her bearings. She shone the torch around in a wide arc and made out the shapes of the logs Demetrius had referred to as the wood supply.

An axe was resting against one of the logs and she had a sudden vision of him swinging it and slicing through the hard wood like a knife went through butter.

She tore her eyes away to peer through the darkness to find the outhouse.

It was where he'd said, right behind the wood heap, its roughly assembled corrugated iron façade looking as if a stiff breeze could easily reposition it to anywhere amongst the surrounding bush.

She shone the torch at her feet as she negotiated the rough path. Once she got to the door she gingerly pushed it open and shone the beam around.

So far, so good.

No red-back spiders that she could see, just an old-fashioned bush toilet like the pioneers had used two hundred years before.

In record time she came back out into the looming darkness and made her way back to the hut, where she could make out the flickering light of the candle and fireplace through the single window.

She had to admit that it did have a sort of appeal if one had a taste for the unpretentious. The hut looked much more cosy and inviting from outside than it did inside, and certainly there was nothing wrong with the fresh air with its slight touch of wood smoke.

Demetrius was stirring a pot of something which was balanced over the fireplace when she came back in.

He glanced at her over his shoulder. 'So you made it back alive.'

She gave him a frosty look and made her way towards the bathroom door he'd pointed out earlier.

She was relieved to find when she shone the torch inside that the bathroom actually had running water. The mirror above the cracked basin had a lot to answer for, however. She could barely make out her features in the speckled glass, the subdued lighting from the now fading torch giving her a sort of ghostly appearance.

She washed her hands and face and looked around for a towel. She couldn't help thinking there was a certain irony in finding two Papasakis Park View Tower Hotel towels folded side by side on a timber dowel against the wall.

She took one and, after drying her hands, buried her head in the soft fabric and breathed in the cleanly laundered fragrance, trying to convince herself that when she opened her eyes she would find herself back in the penthouse and not in the middle of nowhere.

No such luck.

She made her way back to what could only be loosely described as the sitting room for, as far as she could make out, apart from one rickety-looking chair there was nowhere else to sit.

'Would you like something to eat?' Demetrius asked as she came into the room.

'I'm finding myself somewhat hesitant to ask what it is you're actually offering from that cauldron you're stirring,' she said tightly.

His smile looked a hundred times sexier than it should, which she immediately blamed on the flickering candlelight.

'It's certainly not haute cuisine, but edible enough for all that.' He spooned some of the stew on to a tin plate and handed it to her.

It smelt surprisingly good, she had to admit, as she bent her head to inspect it.

'There's cutlery over there.' He pointed to the drawer of the old table in the middle of the room. 'And you can have the chair.'

'I really don't know how to thank you.' Her tone was liberally laced with sarcasm.

The sexy smile was back and she looked away. She had to watch her step with him. He knew all the seduction tricks and a bone-melting smile was trick number one.

She took a tentative mouthful of the food and was relieved to find it tasted delicious, a rich tomato-based meat and vegetable stew with garlic and thyme.

'Some wine?' He handed her the glass she'd abandoned earlier.

She took a sip and watched him take his plate and glass over to the fireplace, where he sat down, leaning his back against one side of the rough mantle, his long legs stretched out in front of him with his ankles crossed causally.

He looked totally at home, she thought—a man who looked as if nothing would faze him, a man who had control no matter what the circumstances. His shadowed jawline only added to his masculine appeal. She could almost feel the rasp of his skin against hers, could imagine the firm mouth seeking hers, the thrust of his tongue into the warmth of her mouth an imitation of what his hard male lower body had in store.

She wrenched her eyes away and took a generous sip of wine.

'How long have you had this place?' She addressed her question to a tiny sprig of thyme on her plate rather than meet his dark gaze across the flickering firelight.

'A few years.'

'I take it you're not much of a handyman.' She gave the room an all-encompassing glance.

The corner of his mouth lifted in a smile. 'I can use an axe and a hammer if I need to but I like things the way they are.'

'Not very progressive of you.'

'Progression has its price.'

She let the silence between them stretch, listening instead to the spit and crackle of the fire in the hearth.

It seemed such an anomaly to her that a man of his wealthy standing would seek such primitive solitude when his money could buy him anything he wanted. No creature comfort was outside his range of income, so why would he come to this backwater lean-to with no modern conveniences? And, more to the point, why had he brought her with him?

She eyed him over the top of her wine glass, wondering what was going on behind those dark, inscrutable features.

A tiny flutter of something indefinable settled in her stomach as she contemplated his possible motives. Did he intend to consummate their marriage? Was that to be her punishment for hiding Kyle? But would it be a punishment? she wondered. Demetrius Papasakis looked every inch the consummate lover; few women would turn down a period of time in his arms, she was sure.

Demetrius captured her gaze and held it within the dark, mesmerising heat of his.

'You look ready for bed.'

'I'm not!' Her face instantly flamed. 'I'm not the least bit tired.'

His lazy smile told her he didn't believe her for a second.

'Anyway, I always read for hours before I go to sleep,' she said.

'Did you bring a book with you?'

She gave him a resentful look. 'I would have if I'd been given enough time to pack.'

'I gave you plenty of time to pack, but you wasted a considerable amount of it arguing with me.'

'And why wouldn't I argue with you? You seem to think I'm some sort of puppet you can make dance at the end of your strings. But I can tell you right here and right now,

Demetrius Papasakis, this is one puppet that is not going to dance to your tune.'

He got to his feet in one easy movement.

Maddison felt herself shrinking backwards in the old chair and, rather than suffer the indignity of falling off it, sprang to her feet and put some much needed distance between them.

His chuckle of amusement irritated her beyond measure. 'You're so delightfully defiant,' he observed. 'Tell me, Maddison, did you play so hard to get with all your previous lovers?'

'That's none of your business.'

'It makes me wonder what it is you're afraid of.'

'I'm not afraid of anything and certainly not you,' she threw at him. 'I just don't want to…to…'

'Have sex with me?'

Her cheeks burned at his words. A vision of her body locked with his flashed through her mind, instantly causing her stomach to flip over.

'I find you the most unappealing lover imaginable,' she said.

A flicker of something she didn't recognise flared briefly in his dark gaze but his voice when he spoke was deep and even.

'What is it you look for in a lover?'

She found his question threatening. What could she say? I have absolutely no idea because I'm still a virgin at twenty-four? How could she admit that to him? How could she admit it to anyone?

She pitched her gaze to the top of his T-shirt so she didn't have to see the satirical glint in his eyes.

'I don't see the point in this discussion for as long as I have breath, I can assure you, the last person on this planet I would ever consider sharing my body with is you.'

There was a small but intense pulsing silence.

'Those are definitely fighting words,' he drawled, bringing her eyes up to his. 'But I wonder if you mean them.'

'Of course I mean them!' She took another step backwards. He closed the distance with two lazy strides, his thighs so close to hers she was sure he would feel them trembling against the rock solid strength of his.

This close she could see the way his dark eyelashes fringed his unreadable eyes, and the way his mouth lifted slightly at one corner in what she was beginning to recognise as his particular version of a cynical smile.

Ever so slowly he reached out with a long finger and traced the smooth curve of her cheek. Maddison felt her breath snag in the back of her throat as the pad of his finger moved to the soft bow of her mouth, lingering over the top curve before moving on in a tantalisingly slow pathway to the fullness of her bottom lip. Her lips began to fizz with feeling and she felt the most incredible urge to take his finger into her mouth and curl her tongue around it, to suck on it, to taste him, to feel him move inside her.

His finger left her mouth to trail a fiery path down the slender curve of her neck, stalling at the front of her top where her breasts lay secretly, shamefully aching for his touch.

Her breathing became increasingly shallow as his finger dipped to the shadowed cleft, lingering there for endless seconds, the heat from the pad of his finger like a brand on her sensitised skin.

His thumb moved over the top of her breast before slipping down to its throbbing peak, which leapt at his first barely there touch.

She saw desire flare in his dark eyes, and her stomach hollowed as his thumb stroked back and forth in a *fainéant* movement, drawing from her an involuntary, barely audible gasp.

She was fast losing ground.

Her legs were liquefying beneath her, becoming boneless and useless as he leaned even closer, his intimate maleness probing her lower body, leaving her in no doubt of his potent arousal.

His head came down and her eyelids fluttered closed, the timeless seconds before his mouth met hers a silent torture of anticipation which she felt in the innermost part of her body where a pulse had begun drumming insistently.

His lips were warm and dry, soft at first, exploring the contour of her mouth with an idleness that was totally captivating. His tongue stroked for entry and without hesitation her lips opened as if he now had total control over her.

He entered her mouth with a deep thrust that sent her head backwards and would have made it hit the wall behind if his hand hadn't moved to bury itself in the thickness of her hair. She felt his fingers thread through the silky strands, her scalp lifting in response to the sensation of having him draw her closer with the firm pressure of his hand.

He wanted access to every corner of her mouth and without demur she gave it to him, relishing the probe of heat as he explored her, drawing her tongue into a seductive dance with his that sent an instant spurt of liquid desire between her thighs.

His body ground hard against hers as he deepened the kiss, the turgid heat of him like a flame to her quivering, traitorous flesh.

She was mindless with her need of him. A need that she hadn't thought possible a few short days ago.

Where was her hatred and loathing now? Where was her anger now that she needed it so desperately to keep him at a safe distance? All had gone up in the flames of desire, a desire so strong she had no way of dealing with it.

It was like a great rushing bush fire that had swept her up into its maelstrom, leaving her no lifeline of escape. The heat was consuming her, drawing her into its molten core until she could no longer think, she could only feel...

Demetrius knew he had to stop before he lost control.

He kept telling himself that was enough, he'd proved his point, but each time he determined he'd break the kiss he'd encounter her soft little tongue, the tongue that had sniped and snarled at him, but now, inside his mouth, was so sensuously tempting, so intoxicatingly alluring, he had no choice but to continue.

Losing control wasn't familiar territory for him.

He prided himself on being able to draw back whenever he wanted; it gave him a sense of safety, his ironclad will the best protection against female exploitation, which he avoided at all costs.

No, these days he called all the shots.

He wasn't the vulnerable sort, at least not any more. It had been a hard lesson, but when better to learn than as a young child? The school of hard knocks was the best place to learn the lessons of life and no one could say he hadn't graduated with honours.

Maddison felt the subtle change in his kiss.

His lips had suddenly hardened, as if he'd come to some sort of decision about what he was going to do with her. It was enough to break the spell of rampant desire as she reminded herself of his ruthless dealings with her over Kyle. She wrenched herself out of his hold with every bit of strength she possessed, and the only reason she managed to escape was because he hadn't been expecting it. She saw it in his eyes as they ran over her insolently, but she refused to cringe under his disdain.

'I think we could safely say I won that round.' His tone was mocking as he drew the back of his hand across his mouth as if to remove the taste of her from his lips.

Hatred seethed inside her where desire had so recently breathed with ragged, gasping, greedy breaths.

'Only because you don't play by the rules.' She glared at him.

'Which are?' He cocked one dark brow.

'How should I know? You make them up as you go. First you say this is a paper marriage and then you try and pressure me to satisfy your detestable needs.'

'Detestable?'

'Not just detestable, but disgusting, loathsome, repugnant, diabolical—'

'I think, you've said quite enough.'

There was an edge of steel in his voice which sent a shower of reactionary shivers down her spine. His expression was nothing short of contemptuous as his eyes raked her from head to foot.

She took in a much needed breath but then wished she hadn't bothered as it seemed to catch at her lungs so painfully she almost choked.

His eyes pinned hers in a look that could only be described as malevolent.

'I'm going outside for a few minutes,' he said. 'During my absence I suggest you prepare for bed. I'll let you choose which side you'd prefer to sleep on, but apart from that you have no other choice. You will sleep in that bed with me tonight; do you I make myself perfectly clear?'

She wished she could outstare him but she was so close to tears she couldn't risk it. She lowered her gaze to the floor and in a voice hardly recognisable as her own answered him in a single softly spoken word. 'Yes.'

She heard him swing away and the sound of the door slamming shut behind him, the sudden movement of air snuffing out the flickering candle on the mantelpiece, leaving her with only the light of the fire to follow the pathway of silent tears down her face.

CHAPTER SEVEN

MADDISON heard him come back into the hut a few minutes later. She listened as he ran the tap in the bathroom, heard the sound of him brushing his teeth and the tread of his footsteps as he approached.

She moved as close to the edge of the bed as she could, clutching the torch like a weapon under the bedclothes.

A single candle burned faintly on the apple carton that apparently served as a bedside table and it flickered in protest when he opened the bedroom door.

She clamped her eyes shut, feigning sleep, but she felt his penetrating gaze all the same. She heard the rustle of clothing and her heart began to thump. Surely he wasn't getting undressed? She was neck to ankles in her heavily pilled tracksuit, fluffy socks on her feet, but if he made up his mind to finish what he'd started she wasn't sure if a full suit of armour would be enough to put him off. She wished she'd thought to wear her mismatched, most unattractive underwear but hadn't had time to think about it in her rush to pack under Demetrius's command.

She felt so tense that she was sure she'd never be able to sleep even if he didn't follow through with his veiled threat.

She felt the depression of the mattress as he got in the bed, his superior weight tipping her towards him. She grabbed the edge of the bed and righted herself but knew her cover was well and truly blown.

'Could you blow the candle out, Maddison?'

She stared at the pathetic little flame, torn with the desire to remove the light source from the room so she didn't have to suffer the sardonic gleam in his eyes, but her inbuilt fear of the dark held her back.

'Go on,' he said.

'Can't we leave it going?' she asked as her fingers curled around the torch underneath the quilt.

He shook his head. 'Afraid not. It could start a fire.'

Oh, the irony!

He'd already started the biggest fire she'd ever experienced inside her own body! The embers of it were still glowing, waiting for the touch of his fingers to reignite them to full heat and power.

His body glowed in the incandescent light, the smooth muscles of his naked shoulders and chest so intensely male she could feel her breathing rate begin to escalate.

She leaned forward and blew out a soft puff of air and the room was instantly shrouded in a darkness so heavy she couldn't see through it.

'It's very dark,' she said unnecessarily and somewhat nervously.

'It's the dead of night,' he answered with a touch of dryness. 'It's supposed to be.'

Her fingers tightened around the torch as she heard him slide down the bed, her body freezing into stillness when a very male leg touched hers.

'Go to sleep, Maddison.'

She held her breath as he shifted his body in the cramped bed, keeping herself as far away from him as possible.

After what seemed like endless minutes his breathing pattern changed and she realised he'd drifted off to sleep.

Her earlier fear turned to frustration.

How could he possibly fall asleep so easily? The bed was too small, the mattress lumpy and with that last turn he'd taken most of the quilt with him, leaving her uncovered and shivering.

It was all she could do not to turn on the torch for comfort. She couldn't remember the last time she'd slept all night without a soft lamp on in the background. She knew it was childish but the loss of her mother when she was ten had turned a habit into a compulsion and now, years later, there was nothing she could do about it.

After another miserable hour or so of fidgeting she finally gave up. She carefully extricated herself from her side of the bed, taking the torch with her to pad out to the sitting room.

The fire had died right down but she gave it a quick poke and placed a piece of wood on the stirring coals.

She sat on the floor, watching as the flames started to lick their fiery tongues at the wood, gradually spreading heat and a warm glow around the small room.

She felt her shoulders gradually begin to relax and settled into a more comfortable position on the old rug on the floor, her head resting on her arm, her eyelids falling…

Demetrius woke to the dawn chorus and stretched languorously. He loved waking up in the bush. The sounds of the wind in the trees, the birdsong, the trickling waterfalls and the clean, fresh air restored his sense of well-being as nothing else could do.

He turned his head and frowned at the soft indentation of the pillow beside him. He threw the bedclothes off and, stepping into a pair of jeans, made his way out to the sitting room.

She was lying in front of the now dead fire, her small body tightly curled as if she didn't want to take up any more space than she needed to.

Her hair was lying in a pool across the floor, a few strands touching her face as if she'd spent a restless night. In one of her hands was the torch he'd given her the night before, and he could see the switch was pressed forward to on even though the beam of light had died out long ago.

He stood watching her for a long time, not really sure why he felt the need to do so but unable to stop himself.

She slept like a child, her cheeks slightly flushed, her mouth open just a fraction, her free hand splayed like a starfish on the floor near her face.

He wondered how long she'd been there, so determined not to share his bed she'd suffered the unyielding cold floor rather than lie next to him. He thought of all the women who'd come to his bed so willingly, and he couldn't help a faint smile. She was so unlike anyone he'd ever met that he knew he was in very great danger of letting his guard slip when he was around her. That was, if it wasn't already too late…

Maddison wasn't sure what woke her but when she opened her eyes she found the sun fully risen and the sound of birdsong filling the fresh morning air.

She stretched and grimaced instantaneously, her limbs feeling awkward and stiff from lying on the rug on the floor.

'Would you like a cup of tea?' Demetrius asked. 'I've boiled the billy and made some toast.'

She struggled up into a sitting position, trying to ignore the pins and needles in the arm that had clutched the torch to her side all night.

'Thank you.'

She took the mug and hid behind its rising steam, cupping her hands around it as she brought it to her lips.

She watched him covertly, taking in his casual attire, the well-worn jeans and the faded sweater, and the heavily shadowed line of his jaw leaving no trace of the well-heeled billionaire in sight.

'I suppose it's pointless to ask if you slept well,' he said.

There was something in his tone that brought her gaze to his. Was it guilt?

'Better than I expected,' she answered dryly, dipping her head to her tea.

He handed her some toast.

'How did you make the tea and toast?'

He pointed to the fire next to her. 'I did it on the fire while you were sleeping.'

She felt distinctly uncomfortable with the thought of him standing so close to where she'd been lying, no doubt watching her every unconscious movement. It made her feel vulnerable in a way she wasn't keen to feel around him. She could only just hold him off while awake, but asleep? What defences did she have?

'Don't look so worried,' he said, obviously reading her look. 'I didn't touch you.'

'I didn't think you would.'

'Didn't you?'

'Surely your deplorable standards wouldn't sink to that level?' She gave him a frosty glare.

It was a moment or two before he responded. 'After you've had breakfast I thought we could go for a walk.'

'Where to?'

'To the waterfall and back. It's a nice walk and if we're lucky we might even see a lyre-bird.'

'If we're lucky we might even find our way back,' she muttered with sarcasm as she bit into a piece of toast.

'I can assure you, Maddison, I know this bush like the back of my hand. I'll make sure you don't get lost.'

She finished her breakfast in silence, not sure she wanted to go anywhere with him except back to civilisation and as soon as possible.

'Have you got comfortable shoes with you?' he asked, taking her empty plate and mug from her.

She nodded and left the room to prepare for whatever form of torture he next had in store for her. It wasn't that she didn't like bushwalking—she did—it was just that there was a long list of people she'd prefer to go with rather than him.

A short time later Demetrius led the way down a roughly hewn pathway which led into the densely vegetated forest, tall trees towering above them, their blue-green leaves trembling in the slight breeze.

She tucked in behind him on the first part of the narrow path, her eyes wandering to the firm shape of his muscled thighs as he stepped over rocks and tree roots. She lifted her eyes another fraction and encountered the tight shape of his buttocks, her mind wandering to what he would look like naked.

It was clear he was no stranger to the gym if the well-developed muscles in his arms were anything to go by, and the ease with which he traversed the rocky incline suggested he was currently in the peak of fitness.

She gave herself a mental shake and forced her eyes to the pathway underfoot, marvelling at the soft lichen clinging to centuries old fallen logs, their craggy limbs in some places reaching across the path as if to caution them against going any further into the deep, dark forest.

She could smell the damp earthiness of the forest floor, filling her nostrils with its clean freshness until she could almost taste it on her lips.

The pathway grew even more shadowed the further in they walked, the silence surrounding them broken from time to time by the flap of a bird's wings as it flew upwards or the snap of a twig beneath their feet.

After a while Maddison could feel the dampness in the air increase, and soon after heard the trickle of water to their left. She peered through the screen of trees and saw the sinuous curve of a creek, its brackish water flowing over smooth river stones that looked as if they'd been finely polished.

Not long after she could hear the roar of falling water, sounding like distant thunder until they got closer and closer, when it became more like a deafening roar.

Demetrius held back a tall frond of fern for her to pass through before him, and as she moved past she looked up and saw the water cascading from a rocky shelf above, the fine spray anointing her up-tilted face. The sound of it falling to the creek below was so loud she almost had to shout when she turned to look at him standing beside her.

'It's beautiful!'

He gave a brief smile and pointed to the top of the falls.

'See up there? There's a rocky shelf we can climb up to and look down at a great view all over the valley.'

She followed his lead and when it came to a particularly tricky spot didn't resist when he offered her his hand. She slipped her hand in his and his warm fingers closed around hers, his in-built strength clearly obvious as he guided her up the rocky slope even though his hold was gentle.

He was still holding her hand when they reached the top.

'Careful,' he warned. 'The rocks here can be slippery from all of the spray.'

She stepped with caution, increasingly glad of his hold as she chanced a look downwards to the creek below.

The rushing water was thunderous in her ears, the swirling vortex beneath them so spectacular she found it hard to recall ever seeing a scene so vitally alive with energy.

The wild water was frenzied in its mad pace to reach the bottom, and once it crashed to the wild whirlpool below, ran on over the submerged rocks and logs with such haste and fervour Maddison wondered how they didn't get caught up and carried on with the force of rushing water.

The cool mountain air was like a restorative drug in her system, she felt as if she couldn't breathe in enough of it.

She brushed at a strand of hair that had come over her face and noticed that the fine spray coming off the waterfall had left beads like tiny diamonds in her loose hair.

She felt Demetrius's shoulder brush hers and his breath caressed her cheek as he pointed into the distance. 'You can see for miles up here. Not a house or high-rise building in sight.'

She followed the line of his vision and felt her breath catch at the scene before her.

The mountain range had a blue tinge to it in the clear spring air, the tall peaks stretching for as far as the eye could see. The landscape seemed endless, without reference to the hustle and bustle of civilisation, the air pristine and the breeze through her hair just like soft fingers in a caress.

Maddison felt something inside her shift and settle.

It had been a very long time since she'd felt anything so remotely akin to peace. The sudden death of her father and her worries over Kyle had taken every ounce of her energy. She'd become so used to the feeling of pressure building to a frantic pace in her breast as she'd tried to deal with the next obstacle life dished out to her that it had taken until now to see how much her inner peace had been sacrificed.

But out here life took on a different context. The soft soughing of the wind through the trees automatically eased her tension, the lacy sunlight through the high canopy gave her a feeling of energy and the sound of the water running over the creek bed filled her head with the symphony of nature unspoilt.

She felt Demetrius suddenly stiffen beside her, his hand on her arm tensing as if to warn her.

She turned her head to look at him, but his eyes were on the path ahead.

'Shh.' His voice was just a whisper of sound. 'Look.'

She looked to where he was pointing and saw a grayish-brown bird. It was scratching around in the undergrowth but it must have sensed their presence for it turned its head and scuttled with the speed of lightning into the thick bush, instantly vanishing from sight.

'What was it?' she whispered close to his downbent head.

'A lyre-bird.' His voice caressed the shell of her ear as he turned to speak to her in an undertone. 'A male one of the Superb species, I think the South-eastern form.'

She felt his hand take hers once more as they continued on, the silence between them not tense now, but somehow companionable. Maddison felt as if something had passed between them in seeing the shy bird. It was like sharing a secret with someone, as it seemed to create an invisible bond between them.

It was a long while before either of them spoke.

Maddison was content to listen to the sounds of the bush around them. She heard the call of birds she'd never heard before in her life, and even the sound of her feet treading the bush path was like a new sound to her ears. The crack of a twig, the crunch of spent leaves and the susurration of the wind through the trees seemed so far away from the concrete towers, frantic traffic and choking fumes of the city.

Demetrius led them even further into the bush, the dappled sunlight above gradually changing to the darker green shadows of rainforest. Rich green lichens clung to every limb of fallen timber and the forest floor was soft with decades of leaf litter which felt like a priceless carpet under Maddison's feet. The air was even richer with the moistness of the earth and the silence beneath the heavy canopy was like nothing she'd ever experienced before.

She stole a look towards Demetrius who was standing with his dark head turned to where a slim arrow of sunlight was penetrating the shadowed forest floor like the beam of a spotlight on a stage.

She followed the line of his gaze and saw a blue wren darting about in the lush undergrowth, his beady eyes noticing their presence but, unlike the lyre-bird, unthreatened by the arrival of company.

'It's a male one, isn't it?' she whispered, coming a little closer to where Demetrius was standing.

His arm brushed against hers when he turned to look down at her.

'Yes, the females are brown in colour.'

'He's not at all shy,' she observed, letting her eyes fall away from his to follow the hopping movements of the little wren.

'No, he probably has no reason to fear us. Very few people come through here.'

A moment or two of silence passed between them.

The wren hopped to a higher perch and, after a few seconds of tilting his head back and forth at them, flew away.

'Come on.' Demetrius reached for her hand once more.

Maddison felt the warmth of his fingers wrap around hers, a tiny *frisson* of sensation running through her hand at his casual touch. She couldn't stop herself from imagining those long fingers on her, touching her, tracing the intimate contours of her body.

The pads of his fingers had a faint trace of roughness about them, as if he wasn't afraid to get his hands dirty doing the sort of outdoor tasks most men in his financial position would never dream of doing. It made her see him in a totally new light. It confused her in a way. She was supposed to see him as the enemy at all times and in all places but now, here, in the middle of the silent rainforest, he didn't seem like the enemy at all.

Now he was much more dangerous to her unprotected heart, much more dangerous than any adversary…

They walked through the lichen-adorned glade to where the creek cut across the path, the brackish water slower this far from the falls, but Maddison still balked at the fallen log connecting the two banks in what appeared to be a makeshift bridge.

'I'll fall in.' She pulled against Demetrius's hold as he stepped towards the log.

'No, you won't,' he reassured her.

She felt the tightening of his fingers around hers and stepped on to the log behind him, trying not to look down at the swirling water beneath.

'How are you doing back there?' he asked at the halfway mark.

'Fine so far,' she said, trying to keep her balance on the log.

'Almost there,' he called out, taking the last few steps.

She was close on his heels, but a sudden movement from the undergrowth on the opposite bank took her attention off her feet and she felt herself begin to topple.

She clutched at the back of his T-shirt even as his hand tightened simultaneously around hers, but the log was slippery and her worn-out trainers inadequate for the task of maintaining any sort of grip. She felt herself slipping and was sure she was going to take him with her, but then he stabilised himself with legs wide apart, his hand around her wrist like a vice as he hauled her up against him.

'I told you that you wouldn't fall in,' he said with a reproachful glint in his dark gaze as it rested on her slightly flustered one.

She could barely breathe this near to him.

His chest was pressed against her breasts, his thighs either side of hers in a bracing position. She could feel the iron strength of his muscles against her trembling legs and the indentation of his belt buckle against her stomach made her acutely aware of how very close she was to him.

'It was touch and go there for a second.' Her voice came out husky and breathless.

She tried to put at the very least some air between their bodies but he held her fast.

'Don't move; that's deep water down there,' he cautioned.

'How deep?' She gave him a worried glance.

'Probably not as deep as what's up here,' he said, looking at her mouth.

She stared at him in confusion, her tongue snaking out to moisten her suddenly bone-dry lips.

'How can there be deep water up here?' Her voice was a bare whisper of sound.

He didn't answer.

She watched as he lowered his head as if in slow motion, his lips coming closer and closer and closer until they were just above hers. She felt her breath tighten in anticipation, her breasts springing to attention against the wall of his chest and her thighs softening between the steely brace of his.

His lips came down to hers, softly at first, tasting her as if committing her to memory. She felt the unfolding of his tongue as it stroked between her pulsing lips, not just asking for entry but demanding it.

She opened her mouth to let him inside and a rush of sensation hit her at the electric heat of his tongue as it dipped and dived to conquer every corner of her trembling mouth.

This was the deep water he was talking about, the sort of water that would drown her if she didn't take great care, she thought as he deepened the kiss even further.

She was trapped in a whirlpool of feeling, too frightened to pull away because of the rushing waters below and yet fearful of allowing the kiss to continue in case she couldn't control her responses to him.

She was already in well over her head.

He had only to look at her with those brown, almost black, eyes and she melted, her tight resolve to hate him at all costs unravelling like a ball of string rolling down a steep decline, leaving her defenceless heart totally unprotected.

She couldn't allow herself to fall in love with him.

She'd be better off falling into the rushing water below; at least then she could swim to safety. But if she were to fall in love she would have no chance, and neither would her brother, Kyle.

Demetrius had already proved how merciless he could be, and if he were to find out she cared for him in any way he would surely use it to achieve his own ends, and those ends most probably would include seeing Kyle go to prison for what he'd done to his boat.

Demetrius's mouth softened on hers and she took the chance to carefully ease some space between their bodies.

He lifted his head to look down at her, his dark gaze far too penetrating for her comfort.

'It's three steps to the bank,' he said. 'And about an hour's walk back to the hut. Think you can manage it?'

It exasperated her that he was so obviously unmoved by the kiss they'd just shared. How could he stand there so casually with his breathing unaffected and his expression so calm?

'Of course I can manage it,' she answered with a touch of tartness. 'What do you think I am, stupid or something?'

Maddison pulled her hand out of his loosened hold with a strength he hadn't been expecting. He made a quick grab but it wasn't quite quick enough. He watched in wide-eyed alarm as she stepped backwards into nothing, falling from sight to land with a resounding splash below.

CHAPTER EIGHT

HE WAS down the bank within seconds but the water had already carried her well beyond his reach.

'Maddison!' He called to her as he stumbled over the gnarled tree roots along the bank, his feet slipping and sliding in the mud. Her head was above water but only just, her hair swirling about her face as if threatening to choke her if the tumultuous water didn't succeed in doing so first.

He saw her hand come out of the water searching for a hold but he couldn't get close enough to offer one. The undergrowth along the bank was dense and mostly impenetrable and, even though instinct warned him against entering the water, regardless of his own safety he plunged into the raging creek.

The water was icy-cold and a whole lot more forceful than he'd expected. He was a good swimmer and his body strong from regular sessions in the hotel gym but it took every ounce of strength to get to her.

He caught her just as her head submerged, the murky brown water trying to swallow her, but he managed to grasp a handful of her hair and haul her upwards.

She coughed and spluttered a full mouthful of water in his face but he hardly noticed.

'Are you all right?' he shouted above the roar of water.

She clutched at him frantically, her eyes wide with fear and her lips already turning blue with cold.

He didn't wait for her to answer; instead he towed her against the current towards the nearest bank, one arm around her as the other reached for an anchor to secure them to safety.

The overhanging branch wasn't as thick as he'd have liked but it gave him just enough leverage to get her out of the main torrent to the more shallow waters along the muddy bank.

He half lifted, half pushed her out of the water before joining her, his breathing heavy, his earlier fear rapidly being replaced by anger at what might have happened if he hadn't made it to her in time.

'You little fool!' he ground out. 'You could have been killed.'

Maddison stared at him from behind the curtain of her mud-encrusted debris-cluttered hair.

He towered over her, his white T-shirt now stained brown and one of his arms dripping blood from a nasty scratch near his right wrist.

In any other circumstances she would have thrown a suitably stinging reply his way. However, her stomach was full of muddy water which she could feel from the bubble of nausea in her throat was intent on making a hasty reappearance.

'I...' She took a gasping breath but could hold the tide back no longer. She leant sideways and spilled the contents of her stomach barely six inches from his feet.

He muttered one short sharp expletive before she heard him squat down beside her, his arms coming around her to support her as the rest of the brackish water left her stomach in heaving, rasping gasps that tore at her tender throat.

'Are you done?' His voice was as gentle as his fingers as they drew back her hair from her face.

'I...I think so.'

She closed her eyes as he pressed her head to his chest, her throat raw, and her pride in tatters.

He felt warm even though he too had been in the water. She pressed even closer, trying to stop the shivering of her body but her teeth were already chattering and her hands felt numb as she clutched at his waist for support.

'Do you think you can walk?' he asked her after a moment.

She eased herself away from his chest and looked up at him with a slightly shamefaced look.

'I...I lost a shoe.'

He glanced down at her feet and frowned.

'You were lucky not to lose your life.'

'D…don't lecture me. I didn't do it on p…purpose.'

'You put both our lives at risk.' He helped her to her feet, his voice still full of reproof.

'You sh…shouldn't have b…bothered rescuing me.'

'Of course I had to rescue you, dammit!'

'I d…don't see why you had to. I would've got out eventually.'

'Yes, on a stretcher with a blanket over your face,' he growled at her darkly.

'And wouldn't you be happy then,' she threw back. 'What perfect revenge for the loss of your boat—my life in exchange for a stupid, overpriced boat.'

'It wasn't a boat, it was a yacht.'

'I don't care if it was a cruise ship,' she said. 'All I know is I had nothing whatsoever to do with sinking it, and I don't see why I had to be dragged out here to pay the ultimate price.'

'All you had to do was tell me Kyle's whereabouts,' he reminded her. 'And I'm not asking you to pay any price.'

'Aren't you?' She gave him a disbelieving glance.

'Tell me where he is and I'll take you home right now.'

She felt deeply ashamed at just how tempted she was to tell him.

She lowered her gaze from the intensity of his and stared at her shoeless foot for endless seconds, fighting to get her failing resolve back into some sort of shape.

'Tell me, Maddison.'

She lifted her chin and met his eyes with renewed determination and defiance. 'I wouldn't tell you even if I were on my very last breath.'

He held her look for a pulsing pause, his expression hardening slightly. 'Your loyalty is admirable but entirely misplaced. Your brother is never going to learn the error of his ways with you acting as his scapegoat all the time.'

'You think I want to spend even a minute longer than necessary with you?' she asked. 'I would've preferred a year in prison myself instead of this ridiculous arrangement.'

She stomped lopsidedly in what she hoped was the right

direction. She heard him behind her but didn't turn around in case he saw the glitter of tears in her eyes.

She would not cry, damn him!

After a while she realised she needed his directions to make it all the way back to the hut and, much as it needled her pride, she had no choice but to slow her pace and turn to him.

'I don't know which way from here.' She indicated the fork in the path with one hand.

'You did well to get back this far,' he said with an ironic glance at her shoeless foot.

She looked down at the wreck of her sock and grimaced. It didn't bear thinking about what state her foot was in beneath the ragged covering of the mud-soaked cotton; she could already feel the burn of a blister on the ball of her foot as it was.

'I have a reasonably good sense of direction,' she said. 'But out here all the trees look the same.'

'There are subtle differences,' he said. 'But it takes experience to pick them out.'

'I'm afraid I haven't had a lot of time available to me to go wandering about like a wild child in the woods.' She sent him an arid look, her tone deliberately sarcastic. 'It must be wonderful to be so rich that you can buy your own patch of wilderness and go and play in it whenever you feel like it.'

'It is,' he answered, his dark eyes holding hers. 'And it's even more fun when I bring someone along to play with me.'

'I suppose you've brought all your lady loves up here,' she retorted with a curl of her lip. 'I can just imagine Elena Tsoulis skipping about the bush in her high heels.'

'Better than no shoes at all,' he returned smoothly.

She gritted her teeth and forced her eyes away from the magnetising force field of his.

'At least I still have one shoe and my self-respect.'

'Your pride does you credit,' he said. 'I admire you for it, actually. Not many women would have coped with what you've just gone through without a fit of hysterics or worse.

But you don't need to feel as if you're at risk of losing your self-respect in your dealings with me.'

'Don't I?'

'Of course not. I mean you no harm, no harm at all.'

'You mean to get me into bed, though. Surely you can't deny that?'

'The thought had crossed my mind.'

His indolent look made her feel as if he had flicked a switch inside her body. Heat coursed through her even though the clothes she was wearing were still wet from the cold water of the creek.

'And if you're honest with yourself you'd admit the same thought has found its way into yours as well,' he added, watching her steadily.

'You've got tickets on yourself,' she said scornfully. 'Anyway, I wonder there's room for any woman in your bed with that monumental ego of yours taking up so much room.'

His laughter was just as intoxicating as his smile and she instantly wished she hadn't triggered it.

She wrenched her gaze away from the dancing light in his eyes but it was no good. The damage was done. She could feel her attraction for him growing with every smile he sent her way. His laughter caused nothing less than a landslide in her heart, tipping her over the edge of reason into a land of dreams that could come to nothing, she was sure.

'Come on, Maddison,' he cajoled. 'Admit it. You're a little bit tempted by me, aren't you?'

She gave him a withering look. 'Chocolate tempts me; you just annoy me.'

He laughed again, which only made things worse. She felt as if he'd just pulled a thin silky ribbon right out of the middle of her heart to coil it around his little finger, pulling her inexorably closer to him.

'You're so cute when you're all fired up.' He smiled down at her outraged features.

'And why wouldn't I be all fired up?' She glared back. 'I'm cold and wet from my baptism in the creek and there's not even a hot shower at that disreputable structure you loosely describe as a wilderness retreat! Why wouldn't I be angry with you? I'm so angry with you I could…I could…' She hunted for a suitable punishment but couldn't think of anything with him smiling at her so disarmingly.

'I'll boil you some water on the fire so you can have a bath,' he offered.

'Funny—' her tone was desert dry '—but I didn't happen to notice a bathtub alongside the cold tapped shower, cracked basin and mottled mirror in your luxuriously appointed bathroom.'

'I have a big basin you could use.'

She stared at him incredulously. 'You expect me to bathe in a mixing bowl?'

'It's big enough for two.'

'Two what? Goldfish?'

'Two people,' he said. 'No point in wasting water.'

'I'm not sharing a bath with you.'

'It could be fun.'

'For you maybe, not for me.'

'You are very definitely underestimating my ability,' he chided her gently with a seductive light in his eyes.

'I'm very sure your ability, as you call it, has left a legion of very satisfied women in its wake, but I'm determined not to be one of them.'

'Determined, but tempted all the same,' he observed.

'Right now I would happily sleep with an axe murderer for a hot shower and a meal that didn't come out of a packet with instructions to just add water.'

'You don't like my cooking?'

'I don't like anything about you,' she shot back. 'I hate you.'

He gave her a long, contemplative look. 'You bandy that hate word around a lot. It kind of makes me wonder if the lady is protesting rather too much.'

She gave him her best fulminating look. 'Would you kindly point me in the direction of your little lean-to so I can get out of these sodden clothes? I'm tired and wet and in no mood to continue this pointless discussion.'

He led the way without another word but all the way back to the hut Maddison felt as if he'd somehow yet again had the last word.

The fire was burning low in the hearth and while Demetrius attended to it Maddison went to the bathroom and removed her wet clothes.

She gritted her teeth under the dripping spray of the cold shower, determined to wash off the mud of the creek in private. She could just imagine the little fireside seduction scene he was probably planning for her but, as tempting as the thought of hot water was in her current state of borderline hypothermia, she was going to do everything within her power not to give in to it.

Demetrius looked up from the water he was bringing to the boil when she came back in. He'd stripped off his wet T-shirt but his jeans were still damp and she was sure she could see steam coming off them as he stood with his back to the fire to face her.

He gave her an assessing look for a long moment before observing with a frown, 'You're still shivering.'

'N...no I'm n...not,' she denied through chattering teeth.

He gave her a you-can't-fool-me sort of look before taking the two strides that separated them. He took both of her cold hands into the warmth of his, his fingers closing over her trembling flesh until she could feel the life coming back into them.

'I'll leave the hut so you can bathe in peace,' he offered.

'I've had a shower,' she said. 'I'll just sit by the fire and thaw out a bit more.'

'Your lips are blue.'

She ran her tongue over them as if to see for herself, but then wished she hadn't when his dark gaze followed the movement with a burning intensity that sent an arrow of awareness straight to her core.

Her desire for him was suddenly like a presence in the room.

She could feel it seeping through the cold layers of hcr skin as if to reach out to his pulsing heat; there was nothing she could do to stop it from leaking out from each and every pore of her body. She felt as if it were written in big letters all over her: I want you, Demetrius Papasakis—only you.

She could tell he knew what she was feeling, for she saw the answering gleam of fiery hot desire leap in his eyes as they meshed with hers in the deep timeless silence that throbbed between them.

Maddison felt her breath hitch in her throat when he drew her closer to his warm frame. His body heat began coursing through her, igniting the fire in her veins, sending arrows of need to every nerve and cell. She could feel the imprint of his arousal against her, the steamy dampness of his jeans against her a heady reminder of her own moistening response to him between her thighs.

She watched in silence as his lips came down towards hers, the soft bow of her mouth trembling not with cold now, but in anticipation of the calefaction of his.

As soon as his lips settled on hers Maddison knew her fight to resist him was more or less over; she had no way of resisting the all-consuming heat of his mouth, no way to escape the tantalizing rasp of his tongue as it searched for hers as a hungry flame went in search for fuel, and no way to stop her heart from beating as if she'd just run the race of her life.

Her response to him both shamed and thrilled her. She didn't understand how she could hate and need him at the same time. It made her feel as if she no longer knew herself, as if she'd turned into someone else with the first brush of his mouth on hers.

She'd felt it the very first time he came to her apartment in search of Kyle. His dark, compelling gaze had ignited something within her, a tiny seed of need had sprouted and grown, spreading like wildfire through her and now she had no hope of containing it.

Her need of him made her reach for him in shameless abandon, her fingers feeling the hard ridge of him straining against his jeans as he leaned into her. His harsh groan into her mouth as her fingers traced him sent an answering shiver of need right through her.

His kiss deepened as he pressed her backwards to the floor in front of the leaping flames of the fire, his weight coming over her, his body pinning her intimately as her thighs shifted to accommodate him.

Their clothes were a barrier but Maddison couldn't help feeling as if they added to the intensity of desire. The straining denim over his pelvis made her all the more greedy to uncover him, and the soft fabric of her top was unable to conceal the proud tilt of her breasts as they swelled under his palm.

She undid the top button of his jeans and slid the metal zipper down with an urgency that belied her inexperience. She was going on pure feminine instinct, relishing the power she discovered she had at her fingertips when he sprang forth in response.

'Oh, God!' He sucked in a breath as her hand shaped him shyly.

His harsh response gave her courage.

Her tentative touch tightened, her fingers lingering where she felt his need was intensified the most. She felt his chest rise and fall against hers as he fought for control, the features of his face contorted with pleasure as she gazed up at him.

Demetrius took charge by removing her hand and securing it above her head, his eyes pinning hers as much as his body.

She knew this was the time to call a halt, but something in her resisted it. Why not? she thought instead. I want him, he obviously wants me, so what's the problem?

The problem was he didn't love her.

She was just a smokescreen for the relationship he valued the most—his affair with Elena Tsoulis.

'You know what's going to happen if you don't tell me to stop, don't you, Maddison?' His words caressed the surface of her lips as he spoke softly above her mouth.

She nodded her head once without speaking.

His black-brown gaze consumed her sapphire-blue one like

a flame licking its way through spilled petrol, lapping her up, drawing her further into the furnace of his blazing passion.

'This wasn't part of the arrangement,' he reminded her as his hand shaped her uncovered breast, the pad of his thumb rolling over her engorged nipple again and again.

'I don't care,' she whispered as she shifted beneath him, searching for the evidence of his need with an instinct as old as time itself.

She found it and felt her spine instantly liquefy at the impact of his hard body probing her searchingly.

'This is supposed to be a marriage on paper.' He spoke just above the swell of her lips, his lower body aching to be surrounded by the tight sheath of hers. 'I shouldn't be doing this.'

'Doing what?' She drew in a snagging breath as his hand moved to the elastic waist of her track pants and began pulling them down, taking her underwear with them.

She felt his eyes on her feminine form, their heat burning through the layers of her skin as if he'd held a blowtorch to her quivering flesh.

'This…' He pressed a soft open-mouthed kiss to the cave of her belly button before moving downwards.

She dragged in some much needed air as his tongue moved over her, separating her delicately, tantalisingly, slowly.

She could barely think for the sensations rushing through her at the feel of his mouth on her, the tightening of muscles unfamiliar to her as his tongue sought the pearl of her womanhood with devastating expertise.

She couldn't hold back her response; it rolled over her in waves of delight that lifted her out of herself on to another plane of feeling. She was floating, then free falling and plunging into a spiral of ecstasy that she hadn't known existed.

Demetrius waited until she had come back down from the heights before he shifted over her and entered her with a single thrust, his breath expelling at the feel of her warm tightness enclosing him.

He felt her flinch and stilled his movement.

'Is something wrong?' He looked down at her, his brow creasing into a frown at the sight of her biting her bottom lip.

She let her lip go and smiled a tremulous smile.

'No…I'm fine…you're just so…' Her words trailed off as her face flamed.

He waited for a moment before moving within her, but as soon as he did so she bit down on her lip once more and to his horror the sparkle of tears sprouted in her blue eyes.

He froze as realisation suddenly dawned.

'Oh, my God,' he groaned and withdrew from her as gently as he could.

She clamped her eyes shut to stem the tears but still they came, trickling down her cheeks as fast as she could brush at them with a shaky hand.

'I'm so sorry,' he said as he got to his feet, reaching for his jeans.

She heard the slide of his zip and squeezed her eyes even tighter.

'Maddison.'

His voice commanded her to look at him but she was too embarrassed. Instead she averted her gaze as she struggled back into her track pants, her hands shaking uncontrollably as she tried to restore whatever dignity she could under the circumstances.

Demetrius stood watching her uncertainly, his brow still deeply furrowed.

'You should have told me,' he said after an agonising silence.

She sniffed and brushed her sleeve across her face in a gesture that totally undid him.

'I had no idea you were…' He let the sentence trail away, still unable to come to terms with his actions.

He pushed a hand through the rough disorder of his hair, fighting for some sort of control.

This was totally out of his field of experience.

He'd been with countless women over the years and not one of them had affected him quite the way Maddison had. It wasn't just the fact of her innocence, which on reflection he knew he should have picked up on earlier, but her whole personality, her fierce loyalty to her brother and her courageous defiance in the face of overwhelming odds.

Guilt assailed him as he looked down at her slim body hunched over her up-bent knees, her eyes avoiding his with all the determination of her nature. For the very first time in his life he knew he was in deep trouble, the sort of trouble he'd so cleverly avoided all his adult life.

Love trouble.

'I don't know how to go about apologising,' he began uncomfortably. 'I must have hurt you.'

She lifted her tear-stained face to his momentarily. 'Only a bit…I'm fine now.'

'I would have taken things more slowly had I known.'

'It's all right.' She bent her head once more.

'No, Maddison,' he said gruffly. 'It's not all right. Do you have any idea how bad I feel?'

She got to her feet with such awkwardness that another shaft of gut-wrenching guilt darted through him.

'Please don't beat yourself up about it,' she said. 'I'm sure there are worse things to feel bad about.'

'Why didn't you tell me?'

'Why didn't you ask?' she returned with a spark of her usual spirit.

He considered her question for a moment or two.

'You're right, of course,' he finally admitted with a touch of wryness in his tone. 'I shouldn't have assumed anything about you. You are, after all, exactly as you said—not like other women, or at least not like the ones I'm most familiar with.'

'Well, no doubt this will be a rather special tick to put in your little black book,' she said.

'You have an appalling view of my character.'

'That's because you have an appalling character,' she tossed back. 'Anyone who resorts to blackmail has to be somewhat deficient in the character stakes, don't you think?'

She'd recovered well, he thought. Her fighting spirit was back with a vengeance, and it seemed she wasn't going to miss an opportunity to get in a couple of well-aimed and no doubt well-deserved king hits.

'You didn't have to marry me,' he pointed out. 'You could have told me of your brother's whereabouts and left it at that.'

'And watch you destroy him as you did my father?' she flared at him. 'Over my dead body!'

'The sacrificial virgin, no less.' One dark brow quirked at her.

She was tempted to hit him, he could tell. He saw the tightening of her fists by her sides and prepared himself for a swinging arc but she must have changed her mind for she simply ground her teeth and turned away.

He was surprised at how disappointed he felt.

A part of him wanted her to hit out so that he could take her in his arms and subdue her. A very big part of him wanted her back in his arms and not just temporarily. He wanted her to reach up to him with love in her flashing blue eyes, not hate. He wanted her to love him the way she'd taught him to love her in the space of days...

'Maddison...' He paused when he saw her back stiffen as he spoke, but then, coming to a decision, continued roughly. 'Pack your things; we're going back to the city immediately.'

She swung back around to look at him, a flicker of relief crossing her face as she saw him begin to damp down the fire.

'We're...leaving?'

'Yes.'

'But...'

'Don't argue with me.' Impatience crept into his tone as he kicked at a piece of charcoal that had slipped from the grate. 'Just get your things and let's get going.'

He brushed past her and left the room without another word.

She stood for a moment or two, staring at the space he'd occupied, the dying fire sending up thin curls of grey smoke into the old chimney in its last choking breaths.

What a time to realise you're in love, she thought.

The fire of his desire was squashed, just like the fire before her, while the embers of her love were glowing inside her, spreading the heat of aching need to every secret place in her body.

She loved him.

CHAPTER NINE

THE drive back to the city was conducted in a silence that was more or less by mutual agreement.

Maddison sat back in the leather seat and stared sightlessly at the passing scenery as it flashed past, a sinking feeling settling in her stomach at what lay ahead.

She cast covert glances in Demetrius's direction but his eyes were fixed on the road ahead, his expression mask-like. However, from time to time she noticed he drummed his fingers on the top of the steering wheel as if he were mulling something over in his mind.

She wondered what it was.

She imagined he was planning how he was going to resume his relationship with Elena once they got back to the city, working out his next assignation with the Greek woman under the guise of his new marriage.

The fierce hot tongues of jealousy licked at her until she had to clench her teeth against their venom.

She had no right to be jealous.

He'd laid out the terms right from the start, even warning her against becoming too attached to the Mrs Papasakis role.

How ironic!

She'd only been his wife for twenty-four hours and she was irrevocably attached not just to the role but to him! How had love crept up on her so stealthily? She'd been so busily stoking the fire of her hatred that the wildfire of love had swept her up from behind, consuming all her resolve, all her rationality and all her reasons for revenge. Her body could still recall his overpowering presence. She squeezed her thighs together to remind herself of what his hard length had felt like, the tug of tender muscles a delicious combination of pleasure and pain.

She felt his glance and met his eyes across the gear lever as he shifted the gears. She wondered if he knew she was thinking about the interrupted intimacy they'd shared and quickly looked away, her cheeks feeling hot and her legs instantly weak.

The car surged forward and she was set back in her seat with a jolt as he overtook a line of slow-moving cars on the motorway.

It was another timely reminder to her of the latent power at his fingertips. He had only to issue a command and the devastation of his power would be unleashed, sweeping up Kyle's future along with hers. But then she recalled his cousin's words at the wedding and wondered again if perhaps Demetrius had a side she'd overlooked. He'd certainly been ruthless in his dealings with her over Kyle but his apology over their lovemaking had appeared both gracious and genuine.

He liked to score conversational points, but surely that came from managing his successful empire. He'd never have survived in the cut and thrust of the business world without a talent for debating the point.

But did he have a human heart beating in that broad chest as Nessa had indicated? Could he be taught to trust and love instead of viewing the world through jaded, cynical eyes? And, more to the point—was she the person to teach him?

Once they arrived back at the hotel, Demetrius's position as both owner and resident became instantly apparent in the speed by which their things were spirited up to the penthouse via the service lifts while the car was valet-parked.

Maddison stood beside him in the guest lift, relieved no one else was there so she didn't have to stand within his embrace in case she betrayed herself.

She felt his solid presence in every cell of her body as he stood silently at her shoulder, his long legs slightly apart, his dark unreadable eyes on the illuminated numbers above their heads.

It seemed the longest lift journey in her life, the pulsing

silence a form of torture to her in her overwrought emotional state.

The lift opened and he indicated for her to precede him. She moved past without a word and waited as he swiped his key card in the lock.

'I'm going to shower and shave,' he said as the door shut behind him.

Maddison brushed a strand of her hair away from her face in what he was starting to recognise as one of her nervous gestures.

'You have your own bathroom so don't think that your privacy will be compromised,' he added tightly.

Maddison didn't know quite what to make of his mood. She sensed a brooding anger in his aloof stance but wasn't sure if it were directed at her or the circumstances that had brought them together.

She pressed her lips together and tried to think of something to say but he got in first.

'For God's sake stop looking at me like that,' he growled. 'I'm not going to throw you to the floor and ravish you.'

She blinked at the rough delivery of his words.

'And don't give me that injured martyr look either.' He glared down at her.

'I'm sorry.' She finally found her voice and her spirit. 'Would you like me to walk around with a paper bag over my head so I don't continue to offend you with my various expressions?'

'That won't be necessary.'

Blue eyes clashed with brown but for once he was the first to look away. He turned on his heel and strode towards the master bedroom, tossing over his shoulder, 'If you're hungry, order room service. I'm going out.'

The bedroom door acted as a punctuation mark on his curtly delivered statement.

'Good,' she said under her breath, fighting back tears. 'Go to your stupid mistress—see if I care.'

*   *   *

She heard him return at three in the morning.

His footsteps stilled outside her door and she held her breath, wishing she'd had the courage to snap off the lamp before she'd gone to bed.

She sensed his hesitation, as if he wasn't sure whether to go in and turn off her light at the risk of waking her.

The seconds pulsed inside her head as she waited for him to decide, but a few moments later when she heard his footsteps move on down the hall she was annoyed with herself for the rush of disappointment she felt.

She turned over to her side and stared at the door as if willing him to open it and come and gather her into his arms and make her properly his in every sense of the word.

She heard the faint hiss of a bathroom tap being turned on and off, and then the sound of his shoes thudding to the floor as if he'd kicked them off impatiently. She heard a swift sharp expletive as something toppled over and crashed to the floor, and wondered if he had been drinking.

The minutes ticked by until eventually all was silent.

Maddison felt her eyelids dropping, felt too the gradual relaxation of tense muscles throughout her body, and the almost imperceptible slide of conscious thoughts into the unconscious...

She woke to the sound of a hacking cough.

With the barest hesitation she threw off the bedcovers and without stopping to pick up a wrap, padded down the hall towards the master bedroom.

She gave the door a little knock but apart from a particularly vicious swear word from inside there was no other response.

'Are you all right, Demetrius?' she called out, leaning in to the door to catch a response.

The door suddenly opened wide. She stumbled forwards in surprise and would have ended up against his chest if he hadn't steadied her with one hand.

He was dressed in a pair of boxer shorts and nothing else, his towering frame intimidating to say the very least.

'What do you want?' he growled down at her as he let go of her upper arm.

Maddison's gaze swept over him in concern.

He was quite clearly running a fever from the flushed look of his features; his dark eyes were dull and his forehead heavily creased as if the morning light was too much for him to bear.

'You look terrible,' she said.

'I don't remember asking for your opinion on my appearance.'

'You're sick.'

'So you've said before.'

She rolled her eyes at him for reminding her of one of her previous insults. 'I mean really sick. I think you need to see a doctor.'

'I'm sure I'll survive.' He leant against the open door, his expression clearly indicating he wanted her to leave.

Maddison stood her ground, her lips set in a determined line as she faced him. He held her look for a moment or two before abandoning the door to turn away, his hand brushing over his face as if trying to eradicate the pain from behind his eyes.

'Have you got a headache?' she asked.

'Go away, Maddison. I don't like spectators when I'm not feeling one hundred per cent.'

'You should take something to bring your fever down.'

'And you should take my advice and get out of here before you catch whatever bug I've picked up.' The tone of his voice belied any concern he might have for her health but she refused to be daunted.

'Go back to bed,' she said. 'I'll get you some painkillers.'

He muttered something under his breath which sounded to her as if he were berating the whole of her sex and not just her, but he did go back to the crumpled mess of his bed to lie down.

She came back a few minutes later with a glass of water and

two of the painkillers she carried with her in her handbag at all times.

'Here you go.' She placed them in the cup of his palm and steadied the glass for him to take a mouthful.

He tossed the pills into his mouth and took a deep draught of the water, lying back on the pillows as if in exhaustion, his eyes shut and his normally tanned face pale.

She reached out her hand and placed it softly against his damp brow, frowning at the heat coming off him.

'You're hot as fire.'

He brushed at her hand as if shooing an annoying fly away from his face. 'Stop fussing, will you?'

'But you're so unwell,' she protested. 'Have you had the flu this year?'

He covered his eyes with the back of one hand. 'No, now go away.'

'Is your throat sore?'

'A bit.'

'Are your muscles aching?'

He opened one eye and glowered at her. 'Get out of here, Maddison. I don't need your little nurse routine, OK?'

She held his glare patiently, as if out-staring a particularly recalcitrant child. 'You need to keep your fluids up.'

'You need to get out of here,' he gritted.

'And maybe something to eat, like soup or—'

The bedcovers were suddenly flung back and he launched out of the bed, stumbling in the direction of the *en suite* bathroom.

She winced as she heard the sounds of him being horribly ill, instantly recalling how she'd felt as the contents of the creek left her stomach the day before.

She pushed open the bathroom door and found him leaning over the basin, his face an even more ghastly white than before.

He turned his head to growl something at her but another bout of nausea hit him and he bent to the basin once more.

Maddison reached for a face cloth and, quickly rinsing it under the shower, came back to press it to the back of his neck.

'Go away,' he groaned but the fight had gone out of his voice.

She wiped away the gathered beads of perspiration in gentle sweeping movements and watched with considerable satisfaction as his tension gradually began to ease.

'This wasn't part of the marriage deal.' He addressed the plug rather than meet her eyes in the mirror in front of him.

'I know,' she said, moving the cool cloth to the furnace of his brow. 'We'll settle the account later.'

He grunted but didn't resist when she moved the cloth over his bare shoulders.

'Why don't you have a shower while I change the bed?' she suggested after a few minutes.

He dragged himself to his feet against the basin and met her clear blue gaze. 'Why are you doing this?'

She rinsed the cloth rather than hold his fevered look. 'It's no fun being ill.'

'Yes, well, I wouldn't exactly call it entertaining watching someone with the flu.'

'I'm not watching you, I'm helping you.'

'You're annoying me, that's what you're doing.'

'*Touché*,' she returned with a pert little smile. 'Now get in the shower while I see to your bed.'

He looked as if he were about to argue about it a little more but then he sighed, stepped out of his boxer shorts and turned on the shower.

It was her cue to leave and, even though she couldn't quite prevent her eyes from dipping below his waist, she reassured herself that he probably was too ill to notice.

He wasn't.

He came out a few minutes later to find her smoothing over the linen of the freshly made bed, her soft smile transforming her face as she faced him.

'Feel better?'

He gave her a grudging nod and sat on the edge of the bed, the towel about his waist slipping to reveal the line of his tan.

He saw the flicker of interest in her eyes even though she tried to disguise it. She appeared slightly flustered as she pulled back the covers, turning her head as he removed the towel.

'I'll…I'll go and get you a drink,' she stammered on her way out of the room.

Demetrius lay his aching head back on the fragrant linen and closed his eyes, but a small smile played about his mouth all the same.

Maddison didn't know whether to be relieved or worried when she returned a few minutes later to find him deeply asleep.

She considered calling a doctor, but when she pressed her hand to his forehead it seemed a fraction less hot and his body was no longer sweating profusely as it had been before.

She drew up a chair next to the bed and watched him as he slept, relishing in the freedom of exploring his features without the disturbance of his penetrating dark gaze.

He was far more handsome than he needed to be, she decided after a long perusal of his aristocratic brow. His square jaw was far too determined, and his mouth much too sensual. His nose looked as if it had received a decent knock some time in the past but its slight irregularity took nothing away from his overall attractiveness.

He turned in his sleep and the sheet slipped, revealing the ridged muscles of his abdomen. She wanted to reach out and trace her fingers along each line, feel the bunching of muscle, the leashed power in his lean frame.

A trail of dark masculine hair arrowed down to where her hands most ached to touch, her fingers actually twitching in her lap as she fought to control the impulse.

She started when his eyes suddenly opened.

'Oh! You're awake.'

He stretched and the sheet slipped another inch.

'What were those pills you gave me?' he asked.

'Just a strong painkiller,' she answered, forcing her eyes upwards. 'Why?'

'They seem to have got rid of my headache in record time. What do you take them for?'

'I need them from time to time for...' She felt the colour leak into her cheeks and lowered her gaze. 'For the occasional bad period.'

She felt the weight of his studied gaze resting on her.

'I thought most young women took the contraceptive pill to counteract those sorts of things,' he said. 'But then, as I recall you telling me on a previous occasion, you are not most women.'

'Sorry to inconvenience you by being so unpredictable.' A touch of sarcasm had crept into her tone before she could stop it.

'You're not inconveniencing me at all.' He lay back against the pillows once more and closed his eyes. 'In fact, quite the contrary.'

She wasn't sure what to make of his comment so kept silent.

After a long pause he opened his eyes again and turned his head towards her. 'Were you serious about your offer of something to drink?'

'Of course.' She got to her feet. 'What would you like?'

'Black tea would be perfect.'

'Would you like some dry toast as well?'

His dark eyes met hers and held them fast for a timeless moment.

'You've obviously been through this routine before,' he observed.

She couldn't help a wry smile. 'Kyle had a bout of glandular fever a couple of years ago. My bedside manner had dropped off a bit till then.'

'There's certainly nothing wrong with it now.'

She told herself she was being ridiculously pathetic for snatching at the casual compliment so gratefully, but she just couldn't help herself.

'Thank you.'

'You're welcome.'

'I'll go and get your tea.'

'Thanks.'

'I won't be a minute.'

'No hurry.'

'I'll be as quick as I can.'

He opened one eye and the corner of his mouth lifted in a smile.

'Stop trying to be polite.'

'I'm not trying to be polite.'

'Yes, you are.'

'I'm not.'

'You are and I can't handle it in my weakened state.' He gave her one of his rare but totally disarming grins. 'I've got used to you being angry at me all the time. You're confusing me with this I-really-like-you-after-all routine.'

She felt a flutter of unease in her stomach. Had she been so transparent?

'I don't like you at all,' she countered. 'I'm just doing what any decent human being would for someone who is suffering.'

Her reply seemed to annoy him for his features closed over and he shut his eyes once more.

'Black, no sugar,' he said, effectively dismissing her.

'Black, no sugar, it is.' She stalked towards the door.

'And dry toast.'

'And dry toast.'

'And Maddison?'

Her hand stilled on the door knob, her gaze swinging back to his. 'Yes?'

'Thank you,' he said levelly. 'I really mean it.'

Her eyes fell away from his as she closed the door behind her without offering a reply.

She paced the kitchen in agitation as she waited for the kettle to boil, her heart racing at the thought of how unguarded she'd been. What had she been thinking? Staring at him so hungrily like a love-sick schoolgirl!

She needed her head read.

He was the enemy, the man who stood between her brother and his freedom. She couldn't afford to let him see how he affected her. If she did, it would surely be his biggest victory. She'd never be able to protect Kyle if he stormed her defences in such a way. She owed it to her brother and the memory of her father to withstand the temptation, no matter what it cost her.

A few minutes later Demetrius sipped at his tea and surveyed the apprehensive features of his wife as she sat nervously playing with the band of her wristwatch as she sat on the chair by his bed.

The toast lay untouched on his plate, his recent bout of nausea making him a little gun-shy of relining his stomach with anything that could make a rapid reappearance.

He pushed the plate away and leaned on one elbow to face her.

'I need you to meet with Jeremy tomorrow,' he said. 'I'm in the middle of a big development deal. He can fill you in on all the details.'

'I know nothing of the hotel business!' She jerked upright in her seat in alarm.

'You don't have to,' he reassured her. 'I just need you to be there in my place. The meeting's at ten tomorrow.'

'But you might be feeling much better by then and—'

'Maddison—' his tone stalled her protest '—please just do as I say. All you have to do is sit in on the meeting and report anything I need to know back to me. Is that too much to ask?'

'No, of course not.' She stared at her hands in her lap. 'I just don't feel all that comfortable with...' She let her sentence die away. Should she tell him of her increasing uneasiness around Jeremy Myalls?

'Good, that's settled then.' His closed eyes and discarded cup indicated the cessation of the conversation.

Maddison got to her feet and, collecting the plate of untouched toast and drained cup, quietly left the room.

She was so aware of him in the next room during the long night she hardly slept.

She heard him use the bathroom in the early hours of the

morning but resisted the urge to check on him. She tossed for hours, wondering if he was comfortable or whether his fever had returned. Finally she drifted off into a disturbed period of sleep where she dreamt Jeremy Myalls had a sheaf of papers he kept holding just out of her reach, a taunting smile in his cold blue eyes as he led her further and further away from Demetrius…

CHAPTER TEN

MADDISON was ten minutes late for the meeting at Demetrius's office due to a last-minute traffic snarl her cab had been caught up in. Demetrius had offered her his car but she'd declined, preferring to make her own way there after she picked up a few things from the pharmacist that she thought might ease his symptoms.

The meeting was well under way when she came in with an all-encompassing apologetic glance around the table as she took her chair.

'Ah, Maddison,' Jeremy greeted her before turning to the men gathered around him. 'Gentlemen, this is Mrs Maddison Papasakis. As you know, Demetrius is currently indisposed with some sort of virus. His charming new wife has been kind enough to sit in on the meeting in his absence.'

No matter how hard she tried Maddison found it impossible not to be intimidated by the boardroom full of men. She seemed to be the cynosure of each and every eye whenever she chanced a look upwards from the sheaf of papers Jeremy had handed her.

After a few tense moments she buried her head back in the documents and tried to follow the main gist of the meeting.

'As you know, the development on the Sunshine Coast has struck some further delays,' Jeremy was saying. 'I have someone working on it presently so those funds will not be represented until the next quarter.'

'Are they being reinvested with the usual people?' a grey-haired man asked.

'Yes,' Jeremy said and tapped the agenda sheet in front of him. 'Now, gentlemen, let's stick to the programme. Let's have your report on the Melbourne refurbishment. Thanks, Stefan.'

It was clear to Maddison's quiet observation that Jeremy enjoyed being in the chairman's role. He seemed to relish the feeling of power the position gave, even though he must surely realise it was only temporary, while Demetrius was ill.

She forced herself to concentrate on the discussion at hand, but when one of the gentlemen questioned a small detail regarding the refurbishment in Melbourne she found her gaze slipping to the financial statement in front of her.

The rows and columns of neat figures reminded her of her father's work, the hours he had sometimes spent at weekends going through the books to make sure every dollar was accounted for.

'What do you think, Maddison?'

She looked up from the financial statement with a guilty flush and met Jeremy's cold blue gaze across the table.

'I'm sorry.' She felt the heat rise up from her neck at the undisguised reproof in Jeremy's tone. 'I missed that last bit.'

It was obviously the wrong thing to say if the frozen stares were anything to go by. She could tell the board had decided unanimously on her not being up to the task and felt annoyed with herself for not concentrating harder, but a tiny question mark had been raised in her head over the investment funds for the Sunshine Coast development. Her father had been working on that account before he died, she was sure. She vaguely remembered him saying something about it being a complicated account due to the amount of money brought in by several private investors who were planning their retirement suites in the luxury hotel resort.

'It's quite clear Mrs Papasakis is distracted about her husband's health,' Jeremy said in what could only be described as a patronising tone. 'Perhaps we should postpone the rest of the meeting until Demetrius is well enough to join us.' He turned to the gentlemen around him. 'All in favour say aye, against— carried.' He snapped his folder closed and the men got to their feet and began filing out of the room.

'But...' She felt tempted to call them back but then thought better of it when she saw Jeremy approach her side of the table.

He pulled out her chair for her as she got to her feet. She felt his hand on her elbow and, rather than call attention to herself by making a fuss, decided to leave it there.

Jeremy waited until the others had left the room before he let her arm go to face her.

'There are a few things I'd like to discuss with you,' he said. 'Privately.'

Her eyes flicked nervously to the door but the last gentleman had already closed it behind him.

'I see.'

Once again his smile didn't quite make the distance to his eyes.

'I thought we might go and have a coffee somewhere.' He paused momentarily before adding, 'I wouldn't want Demetrius to think I'd had you all to myself in the boardroom.'

She knew her cheeks were aflame at the insinuation behind his words but there was nothing she could do to stop it.

'I'm sure he'd understand if it were strictly business,' she responded coolly.

'It's very definitely strictly business,' he returned. 'Your business, in fact.'

There was something in his tone that made her uneasy.

As much as her instincts demanded she get away from him as soon as possible, a part of her insisted she scratch a little more beneath the surface of Demetrius's right-hand man.

She followed him out of the boardroom and once outside the building he led her to a small café with the sort of subdued lighting that made her uneasiness ratchet up another notch.

He waited until a sultry-looking waitress had taken their order before speaking.

'How is your brother enjoying the Northern Territory?'

She reflected later that there were few things he could have said to shock her more. She fought to control the evidence of her alarm by schooling her features into impassivity as if they were merely discussing the capricious spring weather instead of the information she'd struggled to keep hidden at great personal cost.

'I haven't had much contact from Kyle,' she answered with as much evasiveness as she could. 'He moves around a lot.'

'No doubt one does on a cattle station as large as Gillaroo.' His knee touched hers ever so slightly beneath the cramped table.

She decided there was no point beating about the bush, even a bush as large as the sort the Northern Territory was famous for.

'What do you want?'

The coldness of his eyes chilled her to the very base of her spine where it was pressed against the back of the uncomfortable chair.

'I see you're no stranger to blackmail,' he observed with a curl of his lip.

Her earlier hatred of Demetrius seemed to her to pale into insignificance in the face of the depravity reflected in that fabricated smile.

Panic clawed at her insides. What if Demetrius also knew where her brother was? What then?

She sucked in a breath, her hands tightening into knots in her lap.

'I have no money.'

He looped an arm over the back of his chair in a casual manner which irritated her beyond bearing.

'I don't want *your* money.'

It took her a full ten seconds to realise where he was heading.

'But you'll happily take Demetrius's?' she guessed.

He held her hostile look for a lengthy pause.

'I'm offering you a chance to enact your own little plan for revenge. You see, unlike some, I know your marriage to him wasn't entirely your idea. I also know you harbour some considerable resentment towards him over the untimely demise of your father, perhaps not so much as your wayward brother, but enough to want to bring him to his knees if you ever got the opportunity.'

She felt ashamed at how close to the truth his hateful assessment actually was, or at least had been.

She had wanted to destroy him.

She'd wanted to make him suffer for blackmailing her into marriage, but somehow her earlier motivations had been put aside in the last twenty-four hours as if they had never existed.

She loved him, and just as she had done for her brother—would do anything to protect him. She knew she had to be careful dealing with someone as devious as Jeremy Myalls, but if in the end it cleared her father's name it would be worth it, surely? She felt certain now that Jeremy had had something to do with her father's rapid dismissal from the Papasakis corporation, and she was determined to get to the bottom of it once and for all.

She met his malevolent gaze across the table.

'What do you want me to do?'

He smiled a hateful smile of victory as if he'd just landed the biggest fish of an extensive fishing career.

'I'm giving you the opportunity to sabotage his development plans for the Sunshine Coast.'

She swallowed the mouthful of bile his words produced. 'How?'

'I need a bank account to place some funds in. A lot of funds.'

'How many?'

He told her and she blinked. 'That much?'

He nodded. 'That much.'

'For how long?'

He gave a casual shrug. 'For as long as it takes.'

'My bank manager will suspect something. I haven't had more than two hundred dollars in my account for months.'

'Maybe not, but you've just married one of Sydney's richest men,' he pointed out. 'It's quite feasible he would have paid you handsomely for the privilege of sharing your bed.'

'I'm not sharing his bed.'

His eyebrows rose in twin arches. 'So Elena is still in the picture, is she?'

She wished she could tell him differently but what was the point? Demetrius had gone to Elena at the first opportunity and it was time she began to accept it.

'Yes, she's still his…mistress.'

'You surprise me.' His eyes ran over her suggestively. 'I thought Demetrius would've sampled you by now. After all, you've been married—what is it? Forty-eight hours?'

She refused to hold his rodent-like gaze.

'What do you want me to do?' She addressed the stained tablecloth in front of her.

'I just need your bank account number. You can leave the rest to me.'

Maddison scratched out the number of her account on a piece of paper and handed it to him across the table. His cold fingers touched hers as he took it from her and she suppressed a shudder of distaste.

'I knew I could rely on you,' he said.

What could she say?

She was laying a trap just as he was setting his own snare. The only question was, how was she going to get out of it before he did?

'How did you find out where Kyle was?' she asked.

'I have some, shall we say, somewhat underhand connections.' He smiled that loathsome smile once more. 'It's amazing what people will tell you if a little money changes hands.'

She took a ragged breath. 'Does Demetrius know?'

Jeremy's eyes gleamed. 'No, but if you so much as put a foot wrong I'll make sure he does. And we both know what will happen then, don't we?'

She gritted her teeth, not trusting herself to speak.

'I'll be seeing you, Maddison.' He got up from the table and made his way through to the front of the dingy café but it was only after her lukewarm coffee arrived that she realised he'd left without paying the bill.

* * *

Demetrius was awake and in a foul mood when she got back to the penthouse.

'What took you so long?' he growled at her as she set the pharmacist's bag down on the end of the bed.

'I had some errands to run.' She meticulously avoided his eyes. 'I bought some vitamins for you.'

'Vitamins?' He glared at her. 'I don't need vitamins.'

She undid the bag and laid the bottles out on the bedside table next to him. 'Yes, you do. It's obvious your diet is inadequate otherwise you wouldn't have gone down with this bug.'

'People catch viruses all the time. It has nothing whatsoever to do with diet.'

'If you don't eat properly your immune system becomes suppressed.' She opened the first bottle and laid a capsule on her palm. 'We both took a dunking in that creek but you are the one who got sick, not me.'

'So?'

'So your diet must be inadequate.'

'I eat very well.'

'No doubt you do, but hotel food is notoriously high in fat and lacking in vital nutrients.'

'I hire the best chefs, I'll have you know.'

She handed him the three capsules and poured a glass of water from the jug she'd left by his bedside. 'I'm sure you do, but not one of them knows how to cook a decent home-cooked meal.'

'And you do?'

'Of course I do.' She screwed the bottle caps on securely. 'I've bought the ingredients for chicken broth and very soon it will be ready.'

'Why are you doing this?' His brows drew together in a frown. 'Is this part of your plan for revenge?'

She found it hard to meet his hard gaze in the light of the conversation she'd not long had with his second in command.

She pretended an avid interest in the hem of the quilt as she responded. 'You're sick and I'm helping you to get better— simple as that.'

'Nothing is that simple,' he said wryly, 'or at least not where you're concerned.'

'I can assure you I have no other motive than to ensure you are back on your feet as soon as possible.'

'Are you missing your sparring partner?' he asked.

'Not at all,' she answered evenly. 'Anyway, since you effectively removed my place of employment from me I have nothing better to do.'

He'd asked for that but it still annoyed him that she'd flung it back at him. Business was business, and that corner of town was prime real estate; he'd done what anyone with any vision of profit would have done.

'How did the meeting go?' he asked after a slight pause.

'Fine.' She turned away from his penetrating look.

'Did Jeremy fill you in on all the details?'

'He sure did.'

Demetrius frowned at the tone of her voice. 'Is everything all right?'

'Of course.' She sent him an over-bright smile. 'I have the paperwork here for you.' She bent to her bag but his voice stalled her.

'Don't bother. Jeremy dropped it in earlier.'

She straightened from her bag to look at him. 'When?'

'This morning, soon after you left.'

'He didn't say.'

'No doubt he had other things on his mind.'

No doubt indeed, she thought cynically.

'I'll go and get your broth,' she said instead.

'I'm not hungry.'

'It's more fluid than food,' she pointed out. 'You need your fluids.'

'I need to be left alone.'

'And I need my head read for being so patient with you,' she bit out as she got to her feet.

'Maddison?' His voice stalled her at the door.

'What?' She gave a sigh of exasperation and turned around to face him.

She couldn't help noticing how pale he was and how his dark eyes were shadowed as if he hadn't slept properly for days.

'I do appreciate what you're doing for me even if I don't completely understand it,' he said.

'I don't understand it myself,' she said and closed the door behind her.

An hour later she brought him the broth she'd prepared but he sipped at it with little appetite.

She sat on the chair beside the bed with a worried frown between her brows. 'I still think I should've called a doctor.'

'What for?' He pushed the bowl away with a grimace. 'It's a virus. I'll get over it.'

'But you look...so...different.'

'I'm feeling better all the time.'

'You don't look it.'

'I feel it.'

'You're pale.'

'And interesting?'

She couldn't stop her smile in time. 'Yes, you are definitely interesting.'

His lips curved upwards and she was pleased to see the dullness of his gaze lessen.

'You're a tonic, Maddison,' he said. 'I feel better just having you in the room with me.'

Her stomach flipped over at the compliment even as she remonstrated with herself for believing it.

'I think I prefer you sick to healthy,' she said with a little smile. 'You're much more human.'

He looked at her for a long moment without speaking.

'I haven't been all that humane to you, have I?' he finally asked.

She lowered her gaze from the sudden intensity of his. 'You've been...'

'Pig-headed?' he offered.

'Yes, but—'

'And demanding?'

'Yes, but—'

'What about conniving?'

'I don't—'

'Not to mention outright nefarious.'

'I wouldn't—'

'One could almost describe it as Mephistophelian.'

'Mephis—what?'

'Fiendish,' he translated.

'Oh.'

He smiled at her and reached for her hand, his fingers entwining with hers. She couldn't help noticing their warmth, so different from the tombstone touch of Jeremy Myalls earlier that day.

Just thinking about that exchange made her feel guilty.

She felt as if she were betraying Demetrius by even calling his right-hand man to mind, much less agreeing to whatever felonious scheme he had in mind, even though she was determined to sabotage it as soon as she could.

She wanted to tell Demetrius of her suspicions but held herself back at the last moment. She had to go through with her plan to trap Jeremy. It was her best chance of clearing her father's name, and with Demetrius still so intent on avenging the loss of his boat she had no other choice.

'Can I get you anything else?' she asked, sliding her hand from his.

'No.' He rested back on the pillows and shut his eyes. 'You should go to bed; you look tired.'

'I'm not tired.'

'You should be.'

'Why?'

'Looking after an unwilling invalid is tiresome work.'

'I can handle it.'

He opened one eye and swivelled his head towards her. 'I'm beginning to think you can handle most things; in fact, I think I've very seriously underestimated you.'

She shifted her gaze with difficulty, her heart tripping in her chest when his hand reached for hers once more.

He propped himself up on one elbow, his fingers lacing through hers. 'Look at me, Maddison.'

She lifted her gaze to his, her breath tightening in her throat at the intensity she saw reflected in his dark eyes.

'What happened at the hut... I didn't intend to happen,' he began, his fingers idly stroking hers. 'I want you to know that.'

She bent her head to their entwined fingers, her expression slightly rueful. 'Am I so unattractive?'

She felt his fingers tighten momentarily before he tilted her chin up so that she had no choice but to meet his eyes.

'You are one hell of an attractive woman, Maddison,' he said huskily. 'It's taking all my self-control to keep from hauling you into this bed to finish what I started the other day.'

Delicate colour stained her cheeks as she looked at him uncertainly. 'I didn't realise...'

'If you lifted this sheet you'd realise soon enough.' His mouth lifted wryly.

'I...' She swallowed as her eyes flicked to the sheet stretched over his hips. 'I'm sorry.'

'Don't be sorry.' He smiled. 'I think I can handle it—just.'

Here's your chance, she thought, take it.

Don't let a chance at life pass you by.

You love him.

You want him.

Have him.

'Demetrius?' she began in excruciating shyness, her gaze pitched to the fullness of his bottom lip. 'I was...was wondering if...if...' She stalled and the silence dragged on interminably.

'Tell me,' he urged gently.

She sent her tongue out to the parchment of her lips, her gaze flicking to his mouth briefly before returning to his.

'I...I was wondering if you would think it...damn it!' She let her breath out in frustration, her colour high. 'I just can't say it. It sounds so...so...'

'Why don't you show me?' he suggested.

She blinked at him for a moment.

'I think I can handle that—just.' She borrowed his earlier words.

His lazy smile lit a thousand fires in her belly as he bent his head towards hers. 'How about I make the first move; is that OK with you?'

Her single word of assent was lost in the heated cave of his mouth as his lips came down on hers in a kiss that stirred her senses until every rational thought was banished from her mind. She was instantly filled with need, an aching, pressing, muscle-tugging need that she knew only he would be able to assuage.

His kiss deepened as he brought her closer, one hand flinging back the sheet to make room for her in the bed.

She felt the brush of his aroused body against her as she slid down the bed and a rush of feeling shot through her, liquefying her legs and spine at the thought of his possession.

He lifted his mouth off hers a fraction. 'I'm going to take this really slowly so I don't hurt you. Stop me at any point if you don't want to go any further.'

'I'll be fine,' she breathed against his lips. 'Just fine.'

His mouth bent to the neck of her blouse and pressed a hot kiss on the exposed flesh. She felt her breasts tighten in antic-ipation as his fingers slowly released the buttons, her breathing becoming shallower with every movement until her blouse fell apart to reveal the soft mounds to his hungry eyes.

He undid her bra and slipped it away from her body as if it were made of gossamer and not sturdy cotton with one hook missing.

'You're so beautiful.' His mouth closed over one rosy nipple and she felt the delicious graze of his teeth.

'You…you think so?' She sucked in another breath as he went to her other breast.

He lifted his head to smile at her, the warmth of his gaze like a taper on her fevered flesh. 'I know so.'

Maddison felt one of his hands slide down her body to the

waistband of her skirt. 'My underwear doesn't match,' she blurted self-consciously.

His smile widened and her stomach gave a funny little lurch.

'I was in a hurry and I didn't think...'

He traced the soft bow of her mouth with the pad of his thumb, his eyes holding hers in a mesmerising look. 'I promise not to notice.'

She held her breath as he peeled away her skirt and she vaguely registered the soft thud of her shoes hitting the floor as she wriggled out of her tights.

She felt his mouth on her belly button, his tongue dipping in, rolling once or twice before coming out to move further down her body.

She could feel the warmth of his mouth on her intimately through the thin fabric of her panties, the barrier of worn lace only increasing her need of him as his tongue traced her delicate form.

He removed the lace with such painstaking slowness she felt every wrinkle of fabric as it slid along the length of her thigh in a tantalising caress, elevating her awareness of her body to yet another height.

He moved over her, his chest coming to hers in a depression of solid weight she found intensely arousing. She felt the nudge of his engorged flesh against her and her thighs folded outwards instinctively as he settled between them.

He parted her with his body, gliding through to wait until she was ready for more of him.

'Am I hurting you?' he asked against her mouth.

'I think I can handle it.'

'Tell me if it gets too much.'

'It's not too much.'

He moved another fraction and she felt her body clench around him, the tender muscles tentative at first until they became accustomed to his hard presence.

He deepened his entry and she clung to him with a gasping breath of pleasure, her body relishing the feel of his intimate invasion.

He started a slow rhythm of movement, waiting until he was sure she was comfortable before increasing his pace.

Maddison felt herself being carried away on a tide of building delight, an exquisite tension drawing all her nerves into a tight ball tottering on the edge of release.

Demetrius slipped his hand between them to heighten the spiralling sensations he could feel rippling through her, relishing the sound of her breathless little gasps that felt like caresses on his skin where her head was pressed against his shoulder.

'Let go, Maddison,' he said softly. 'You can do it; let yourself go.'

The tight spiral was at breaking point, she could feel it in each and every cell of her body as his next deep thrust finally tipped her over. She was falling, swirling about in a whirlpool of feeling, her high cries of rapture a totally new sound to her ears.

He could wait no longer.

With a deep groan he surged one more time to bring himself the release he craved from the tight cocoon of her body.

Maddison felt the force of his pleasure as he exploded inside her, his large body becoming almost limbless as he finally collapsed in spent desire.

She felt the rise and fall of his chest against hers, his body still within her as if he didn't want to be the first to break the union. Her skin felt tingly as if every nerve had risen to the surface of her body in search of his caress, and she wondered if it was normal to want him again so soon. Was she so insatiable, so wanton?

She felt him shift his weight to look down at her.

'Are you all right?'

'I'm fine.'

'Not sore?'

She shook her head.

He pressed a soft kiss to her mouth and she felt the first stirrings of his renewed desire inside her where he still lay so intimately enclosed.

He caught her surprised look and smiled. 'See what you do to me?'

'Is it too soon?' she asked.

'I think I can handle it—just.' He grinned and captured her mouth with his.

CHAPTER ELEVEN

MADDISON decided much later that evening that it would be so temptingly easy to pretend they had a normal marriage.

She was lying in the circle of Demetrius's arms; his body was relaxed in the deep sleep of satiated desire, his long legs interlaced with hers, his chest at her back a solid, comforting warmth.

She could imagine anyone looking in would naturally assume that love was the tie that bound them together when nothing could have been further from the truth.

She was in no doubt of his desire for her, but at no time had he declared any other feeling for her. The reasons for their marriage remained. He'd wanted recompense for the loss of his boat and she had been the payment in lieu of her brother.

It certainly didn't bode well for a lifetime of happiness, she reflected sadly. Her brother's guilt was a chasm between them even if she did manage to clear her father's name.

She hated thinking about her meeting with Jeremy Myalls. It made her feel contaminated, as if his sly nature would somehow rub off on her in her dealings with him. But she didn't see that she had any choice other than to play his game for a while so she could in the end subvert his devious ends.

She'd reconsidered telling Demetrius about Jeremy's perfidy but seriously wondered if he'd believe her. Jeremy had worked for him for years, and with the cloud of guilt hanging over her father's memory, not to mention Kyle's track record of minor offences, she couldn't see how he'd be all that convinced.

No, she'd have to show him through other means, even if it meant getting her hands a little bit dirty.

She felt Demetrius stir behind her, his warm breath caressing the bare skin of her shoulder.

'Aren't you going to turn off the light?' he murmured, his lips nibbling at her neck.

'Can't I leave it on?' she whispered back softly, shivering as his mouth moved to her earlobe.

He turned her onto her back in one easy movement, leaning over to trail a pathway of soft kisses along the shadowed valley between her breasts.

Her breath caught at the sight of his dark, tousled head buried between the creamy globes of her flesh, his hot mouth sliding along to capture the already tight nipple.

He left her breasts to move down her quivering body, lingering over her stomach before moving to the secret pool of need he'd reawakened between her thighs.

She clutched at his dark curls as he found his target, wave after wave of feeling rushing through her, leading her to that high pinnacle once more.

She made it to the top in deep, gasping breaths, the delicious spasms of ecstasy rocketing through her until she was entirely boneless.

He slid back over her, his warm palm covering her breast as he looked deeply into her passion-slaked eyes.

'You're so responsive; I don't think I'll ever get tired of making love to you.'

Oh, how she wished she could believe him!

'What about Elena?' she asked, before she could stop herself.

His eyes hardened a fraction, but his expression gave absolutely nothing away. 'I would prefer it if you would decline from discussing my relationship with Elena until we are out of bed.'

'Three's a crowd?'

He held her cynical look for a whole lot longer than she could cope with. She felt the sting of tears at the back of her eyes, which made her even more reckless.

'Don't tell me you're feeling a bit guilty?'

'Not at all.' His hand on her breast tightened marginally. 'I told you earlier I would have my cake and eat it too.'

'Yes.' Her eyes flashcd at him angrily. 'But I didn't realise then that I would be the icing on the cake.'

His lower body made its presence felt against the softness of hers. It shamed her that her body had welcomed him so flagrantly, with such wanton abandon and such pressing, desperate need.

She felt herself being pinned backwards under the hastening movements of his body within hers, his own driving need carrying her along in its wake.

She felt him in every deepening stroke, her tender muscles faintly protesting at the urgency and speed, but unable to call it to a halt so great was her desire for him.

There was an element of ruthlessness in his lovemaking. His hands had lost their gentleness, but it did little to stem the flow of rising passion which was threatening to totally consume her.

He made her beg.

For that she almost hated him.

She sobbed out her need for him as he held her just beyond it, drawing out her response until she lost all sense of pride and cried and pleaded with him to let her go over the edge to the paradise she craved.

His answering grunt of satisfaction when it followed so closely on the heels of hers should have been enough consolation to her but somehow wasn't.

She lay spent in his arms, his dark eyes boring into hers with the light of savage victory in his gaze.

'I hate you,' she said, her breasts brushing his chest with every ragged breath she took in.

His lip curled sardonically. 'I thought you might.'

She ground her teeth, wishing she could deny it. 'I'd like to sleep in the other room.'

'No.'

'I want the light on.'

'No.'

'I need the bathroom.'

'Nice try.'

'I mean it.'

'I'll come with you.'

'No!' She glared at him. 'Am I to have no privacy?'

His eyes held the faint trace of a smile. 'Go on then.' He rolled away to lie back with his arms propped behind his head, his nakedness quite clearly of no concern to him.

She tugged at the sheet to cover herself but it wouldn't give an inch under his weight. She sent him a furious look and, reaching for the single lamp, snapped it off.

'Now you can't see me,' she said and made her way somewhat blindly towards the door.

'Maybe not,' he called after her, his deep voice like velvet. 'But I can still feel and taste you.'

She closed the door behind her, but all the way to the bathroom she felt his presence between her trembling thighs and she could still taste him on her lips and tongue.

Demetrius was awake before her the next morning. She opened her eyes to find him standing beside the bed, dressed in a business suit, no trace of illness about him.

She struggled up into a sitting position, gathering the sheet around her, her eyes widening at the time shown on the bedside clock.

'Why didn't you wake me?'

'I saw no need to.'

She forced herself to meet his studied gaze. 'Have you recovered?'

'Remarkably.'

His eyes glinted meaningfully and she lowered her eyes to the sheet edge she was absently plucking between nervous fingers.

'What will you do today?' he asked when she didn't speak.

'I don't know.' She let the sheet go and looked at him. 'What am I allowed to do?'

'You know the rules.'

'No fraternising with the staff, no flirting or sexual encounters… What else is there?'

'You're allowed to shop.'

'Shop?'

'Yes, that activity where money is exchanged for goods. You might get to like it after a while; most women do.'

'I'm not most—' she began but his finger came down and pressed against the soft surface of her lips.

'I know. I've heard it before—you're not like most women.'

There was an ironic tinge to his tone which made her feel as if he were reminding her she'd given in to his seductive charm as no doubt most women had done in the past, and were very likely to keep on doing in the future.

'I'll call you later.' He dropped a swift kiss to the petulant bow of her mouth before moving away to the door.

She folded her arms across her chest and poked her tongue out at his back.

'Behave yourself, Maddison. Remember I'm watching you,' he said without turning around.

A tiny flicker of unease passed through her stomach at his words. Had he some sort of sixth sense where she was concerned?

'How could I forget,' she muttered as the door closed behind him.

In the end she decided to do as he suggested and go shopping. She brandished the credit card he'd given her, trying not to wince at the amount of money she was clocking up as the morning progressed.

She sent her packages back to the hotel in a cab and wandered about the city for another hour or two, wondering how she was going to fill the rest of the day.

Eventually she found her way to the National Art Gallery and spent a couple of quiet hours roaming about the priceless works of art, the formal silence of the colonial building a welcome relief after the frenetic pace of the city.

She left the gallery and continued on through the Domain until she came to the Botanic Gardens, stopping at the very place where she'd agreed to become Demetrius's wife less than a week ago.

How things had changed!

She was his wife in every sense of the word, but for how long?

How could she live with him indefinitely with her brother's guilt still suspended between them?

How could she continue with a marriage that had only come about through blackmail?

How long would it take before Demetrius called her brother to account for his behaviour even though he'd said Kyle's slate would be clean upon her marriage to him?

Could she trust him to keep his word? Especially now he'd consummated their relationship after having reassured her he wouldn't?

She chewed her lip in agitation as she walked through Hyde Park back to town, a hundred worrying thoughts taking up her concentration.

She didn't see Jeremy until it was far too late to avoid him.

He was on the opposite corner, waiting for the lights to change, his cold blue eyes instantly seeking hers, that loathsome smile curling his thin lips.

She considered making a run for it but knew somehow he'd enjoy the thought of having rattled her in such a way. Instead, she waited where she was as if they'd arranged to meet on that particular corner at that specific time.

'Hello, Jeremy,' she got in first.

'As always it's a pleasure to see you, Maddison.' His eyes wandered over her in a leisurely manner. 'Fancy another coffee?'

'Only if you are paying,' she answered.

He ignored her little jibe and took her arm and led her to the café on the edge of the park. She suffered his hold in order to avoid drawing unwanted attention; she wanted this meeting to be over quickly.

She sat on the chair he pulled out for her and, smoothing her irritated features into more passive lines, faced him with the imitation of a smile on her face.

'How is your plan going?' she asked.

'Very well,' he replied. 'Demetrius suspects nothing.'

'Have the funds been relocated?'

'The transaction will go through in the morning. This time tomorrow you will be a very rich woman, albeit temporarily.'

'Why not redirect the funds to your own account?'

'That's way too obvious.' He gave her a sly look. 'That would be the first place Demetrius would look.'

'How long do you expect the funds to be in my account?' she asked.

'Not long.'

'Aren't you a little concerned I might take myself on a shopping spree?'

His cold snake-like eyes snared hers. 'If one cent of that money goes missing Demetrius will be immediately informed of your brother's exact location to the very last square inch of land he is standing on.'

'What do I get out of this deal?' she asked.

'You get to enjoy making Demetrius regret he ever married you. A suitable reward, don't you agree?'

It sickened her to have her previous promise to Demetrius thrown back at her via his corrupt second in command.

'Yes.' She carefully avoided his gaze. 'I shall enjoy every minute.'

'Good girl.' He touched her hand with one of his. 'I knew I could trust you. After all, you and I have a lot in common— we both hate Demetrius.'

Oh, how she wanted to deny it!

'Why do you hate him so much?' she asked once their coffee had arrived.

He leaned back in his seat, one hand stirring his coffee as he surveyed her face.

'He took the one woman I loved away from me.'

She hoped she wasn't going to get a detailed account of yet another of Demetrius's conquests, but sensed Jeremy was going to give it all the same.

'He had no need of her.' His expression soured. 'He used her like every other woman he's been involved with.'

She could hardly argue with that; she'd more or less been a pawn in Demetrius's game of revenge right from the very start.

'He'll do the same to you if you fall for his particular version of charm,' he warned. 'And when he's finished playing with you he'll spit you out the corner of his mouth.'

'I'm sure I'll manage to withstand the temptation.'

'You'd better. If he gets wind of what you're doing with me there'll be hell to pay.'

'He won't hear about it from me.'

'No, I imagine not.'

A tiny silence fell between them.

Maddison disturbed a few grains of sugar on the tablecloth in front of her, unable to stop thinking about the very real possibility that Demetrius would somehow come to hear of her supposed duplicity.

She lifted her troubled gaze to meet Jeremy's briefly.

'I take it you suffer no fear over Demetrius finding out about your devious plan for revenge?'

'No fear at all,' he said. 'I'll be thousands of kilometres away by the time he gets wind of it.'

Not if I can help it, she thought.

'He's a very astute person,' she pointed out. 'He might already suspect something.'

'He's been too preoccupied with his mistress.'

That was another point she wished she could argue over but couldn't.

'I feel uneasy about all this,' she admitted, hoping to put him off the scent of her own double dealing.

'Don't worry, I've got it planned down to the finest detail. All you have to do is pretend everything is normal while I work in the background to bring about our plot for revenge.'

What was normal about any of this? she wondered. She was agreeing to a scheme that could just as easily blow up in her face if it didn't go according to her plan.

'I still think you're underestimating Demetrius,' she said.

'You worry too much. He knows nothing, believe me. He

leaves all the finer details to me, has been doing so for years. How else did I get away with that little affair with your father?'

A serpent of hatred coiled in her belly at the callous way he'd mentioned her father.

'You set him up, didn't you?'

'He was a sitting duck, Maddison. He thought he knew all the ropes but I had something up my sleeve.'

'How did you do it?'

'It was easier than I thought. Your father needed some money in a hurry; I believe it might have been to pay off one of your brother's numerous debts. I set up a short-term loan from the company.'

'Without Demetrius's knowledge?'

He gave her a fabricated smile. 'Of course.'

'And you called in the loan before he could repay it.' It wasn't a question, more of a statement.

'He got panicky, thought I might spill the beans.'

'So you twisted the screws?'

'Only a bit.'

'Enough to bring on a heart attack.'

'Now, now.' He tapped the back of her hand reprovingly. 'Don't forget it was Demetrius who fired your father, not me.'

She couldn't forget it but she wondered if Demetrius would have done so if he'd known about the loan arrangement.

Compassion wasn't a quality she readily associated with him, but somehow she couldn't help thinking he might have done something to ease the financial pressure on her father if he'd known what had been going on.

'I have to go.' She got to her feet. 'Demetrius will be wondering where I've got to.'

He followed her out of the café, stopping briefly to throw some money on the counter for the coffees. Maddison wished she could shake him off but knew any sign of her uneasiness would make him suspicious. She was in so deeply now she had no choice but to follow it through, even though everything within her revolted at the thought of what she had committed herself to.

He walked with her to the southern end of the park, throwing her a conspiratorial wink as he darted through the congested traffic to get to where he was going.

Maddison stood staring after him for a few moments, waiting until he was out of sight before turning towards the hotel.

Her packages had arrived earlier and she spent the remainder of the afternoon unpacking the clothes she'd bought into the wardrobe in the spare room.

She hadn't allowed herself to think about whether Demetrius would want her to move into his room. Better to leave things as they were to avoid disappointment.

He came home just as she was putting the empty packaging in the bin under the sink.

She turned as he entered the room, her hands twisted together in front of her, her expression a lot more flustered than she'd have liked.

'Hello.'

He put down his briefcase and keys before striding across to where she was standing. 'Hello to you,' he said, touching her mouth with his in a brief but heady kiss.

'How have you been feeling today?' she asked.

'Such wifely concern,' he drawled.

'If you don't wish me to act as a wife in private and in public you have only to say,' she said crossly. 'I can assure you it won't matter in the least to me.'

He hitched up her chin with a long and very determined finger. 'Still mad at me?'

Still mad about you, she wanted to say but knew she couldn't.

She held his look but knew her eyes were brightening with tears as every pulsing second passed.

After a long moment his thumb rose to the edge of her eye and tracked the pathway of a crystal tear under its warm pad.

'Don't cry, Maddison.'

His gentle tone was her undoing. She felt her bottom lip tremble and the tears began in earnest, sliding down her cheeks until she could barely see.

Demetrius pulled her into his chest, his hand resting on the back of her head to hold her close.

'I wondered when this was going to happen.' His voice rumbled under her cheek.

'You push me too far,' she sobbed.

'I know I do.' He threaded his fingers through her hair. 'I can't seem to help it.'

He held her from him so he could look down at her.

'Why don't we call a temporary truce?'

'Why temporary?' she asked with a little sniff.

'I don't like long-term promises,' he said, pulling out his handkerchief and handing it to her. 'I find them hard to keep.'

She wondered if this was some sort of clue to the family background his cousin Nessa had alerted her to.

'Well, I don't like short-term commitments,' she said with an element of recovered pride. 'It seems to suggest a lack of trust.'

'Trust is yet another one of those things one has to earn rather than assume as a given,' he pointed out. 'But who knows? Maybe in time I'll change my mind.'

'Is there anyone you do trust?'

He thought about it for a long moment.

'I think it's imperative to trust the people with whom you work closely. I know you don't understand it, but that's one of the reasons I had to let your father go—I no longer trusted him.'

Oh, the agony of not being able to clear up that little detail!

'So—' she fiddled with one of his shirt buttons, fastidiously avoiding his eye '—Jeremy Myalls has quite clearly earned your trust. How did he manage to do that?'

'Jeremy has worked for me for years. He's had more opportunity than most to exploit my faith in him, but so far he has conducted himself in a trustworthy manner.'

'You say that as if you haven't quite ruled out the possibility that he might disappoint you at some stage.'

'I have found from past experience that most people disappoint you in the end. The trick is not to let it show how it gets to you.'

Another clue, she thought.

'Who has disappointed you the most?' she asked, lifting her gaze to his.

He put her from him and, moving a few steps away, wrenched at the tie at his throat as if he were trying to get rid of a noose around his neck.

'Why all the questions?' He frowned. 'You're starting to sound like something out of a how-to-really-talk-to-your-husband manual.'

'Reading one mightn't be such a bad idea,' she retorted. 'I hardly know you at all.'

'Did I ask you to get to know me?' He glared at her. 'I asked you to marry me for a period of time, that's all.'

'I don't like sleeping with strangers.'

'You don't have to sleep with me.'

'Fine by me.' She folded her arms across her chest.

He gave her a narrow-eyed look. 'What's all this about, Maddison?'

'What's all what about?'

'This.' He waved his arm to encompass them both. 'I thought we'd moved beyond taking pot shots at each other.'

'Just because you've had sex with me doesn't mean I have to automatically agree with everything you say.'

'I'm not asking you to. I just want you to fulfil your part of the arrangement.'

'For how long?'

'For as long as I say.'

'So once again you get to call all the shots.'

'If you have a problem with that you know how to fix it.'

'You said that once I married you Kyle's slate would be clean as far as you were concerned.'

'Did I?' He arched one brow. 'Why don't you tell me where he is to see if I'm a man of my word?'

'I wouldn't trust you as far as I could smell you.'

'You're seriously underestimating the strength of my after-shave, not to mention my determination to see justice served.'

She swung away from his arrogant look and fought with herself to keep control.

'Go and get dressed in something other than one of those disreputable tracksuits you seem to favour,' he said after a tense little silence. 'We have a dinner engagement this evening.'

She turned back round to face him. 'I'm not going out with you.'

'I'm sorry to disappoint you, but indeed you are.'

'You can't make me.'

'Do you want to test that little theory of yours?' he asked. 'I'm more than willing, and you know from experience I'm more than able.'

'You are the most arrogant man I've ever met!'

'Maybe, but since we're trading insults you are the most exasperating woman I've ever had to deal with. You go from tears to temper in the matter of seconds.'

'That's because you make me so angry!'

'You make me furious, so at least we're square.'

'I detest you.'

'Right now, you're not exactly on top of my favourite people list either.'

He had the last word yet again.

His words had stung her rather more than she cared to admit, but even as she turned on her heel and stalked from the room deep down she knew her anger was really directed at herself rather than him.

Her need to know more about him as a person sprang from her love for him. She wanted him to learn to trust her, but she couldn't see that happening with him becoming so prickly as soon as she began to scratch the surface of his background.

The irony was that he trusted the one man he shouldn't be trusting. Her desire to inform him of Jeremy's duplicity was overruled by the thought of what Jeremy would do in retaliation. If only she could be sure Demetrius would leave Kyle alone if he were to be informed of his whereabouts, but could she trust him that far?

She couldn't risk it, at least not yet.

Once she cleared her father's name, Demetrius might be more willing to listen and renegotiate regarding Kyle's future, but until then she had to keep silent.

All she had to do was to wait until the money was deposited in her account tomorrow and withdraw it soon after, ready to hand back to Demetrius. In less than twenty-four hours she would be free of the poison of Jeremy's threats.

All she could do was wait.

She had no other choice.

CHAPTER TWELVE

MADDISON came out of the spare bedroom dressed in her new pink chiffon evening dress, her make-up subtle and her hair on top of her head in a casual but elegant knot.

She felt Demetrius's gaze sweep over her in unashamed male appraisal, making her stomach instantly free fall in reaction to the raw desire she could see reflected there.

'Shall we go?' He hooked up his jacket with one finger as he shouldered open the door.

She stepped past him, conscious of her dress drifting across his hard-muscled thighs as softly and seductively as a caress.

All the way down in the lift she felt as if her air supply had been reduced; each breath she drew in seemed to catch somewhere in the middle of her chest.

Demetrius was silent.

He stood watching the numbers descend, his expression now unreadable although Maddison felt sure she could see a tiny nerve beating at the corner of his mouth.

The lift hissed open and he took her arm and drew her close to his side as they made their way past reception to the waiting car.

He didn't speak until they were more than halfway across town. 'I was serious about what I said earlier about a truce.'

She sent him a cautious glance, her hands clasping her evening purse in increasing nervous tension.

'But only a temporary one, right?' she asked.

He gave a small shrug as he took the Neutral Bay exit.

'Neither of us is very good at keeping our responses to each other under control,' he pointed out wryly. 'But if we take it a day at a time, who knows? We might actually make it through a week or two without a showdown.'

'I'm not sure why you want to call a cease-fire.' Her brow furrowed as she fidgeted with the clasp of her purse.

It was a full minute before he asked, 'Have you ever considered what our relationship would have been if we hadn't met under our current circumstances?'

Maddison wasn't sure how to respond to such an unexpected question. What would she have thought of him without the issue of her father and Kyle to colour her earlier judgement?

'No,' she answered flatly, unwilling to commit herself. 'I've never thought about it.'

She felt his glance slant her way but didn't turn towards him.

'Why don't we pretend just for tonight that we've just met,' he said.

'You can't be serious.'

'Why not?'

'Because…' She sent him a worried look. 'I'd feel stupid, that's why.'

'Let's give it a trial run,' he suggested as he deftly parked the car.

'How do you mean?' Her hand hovered uncertainly over the seatbelt fastening as if she wasn't sure if should get out of the car or not.

He held out a hand to her and somehow her fingers slipped into its warm grasp. 'Hello, Maddison Jones.' He smiled that thousand watt smile. 'My name is Demetrius Papasakis. Would you have dinner with me tonight?'

'I…' She swallowed the constriction in her throat and began again. 'Yes, I will have dinner with you.'

His smile lit his eyes and she felt her mouth curving upwards in spite of her earlier misgivings.

He escorted her to the restaurant without touching her, although she felt as if she'd never been more acutely aware of him. His long stride shortened to match hers, his lean muscled arms loose by his sides, his shoulder as close as it could be without actually making contact.

The waiter seated them in a quiet corner of the restaurant and after taking their drinks order moved away discreetly.

Demetrius leaned back in his chair and surveyed her face for a moment.

'Tell me about you, Maddison Jones.'

'Me?' It came out more of a squeak.

'Yes.' He smiled with his eyes. 'You.'

'I…' She sent her tongue out to her dry lips. 'I'm not sure I'd be all that interesting to someone…like you.'

'You don't know me, so how do you know what interests me?'

'I don't know. I guess I was thinking someone with your sort of…background would find someone from mine a bit boring.'

'Why not test me and see?'

She couldn't hold his intense gaze and lowered her own to the glass of champagne the waiter had just set down in front of her.

'All right.' She toyed with the stem of her glass. 'I guess I had a more or less happy childhood until my mother died when I was ten. After that, things were never quite the same, even though my father was so devoted and did his best to be there for us.' She lifted her eyes to his and was surprised to find how warm they looked. 'Us being my brother, Kyle, and I,' she continued. 'He's five years younger than me and, to be truthful, a bit of a handful.'

'How so?'

She ran her finger around the top of her fizzing glass reflectively.

'Ever since he got into his mid to late teens he's run a bit wild. You know, the usual stuff, underage drinking, shoplifting, car stealing and…'

'And?'

She caught her bottom lip between her small white teeth.

'You can tell me. I won't tell anyone,' he put in.

She let her lip go to smile at his dry sense of humour. 'Boat sinking.'

'Boat sinking?'

She gave him a rueful roll of her eyes. 'Yacht sinking, to be precise.'

'Even worse.'

'Definitely much worse.'

There was a funny little silence.

'What about you?' she asked, picking up her glass and bringing it towards her mouth. 'Have you got any brothers or sisters?'

He shook his head as he reached for his own drink.

'I'm an only child. My parents divorced when I was young.'

'How young?'

Maddison noticed his fingers tightened around his glass but his expression remained mostly detached, as if he were discussing someone else's history, not his own.

'Five.'

'That's very young,' she said softly. 'Who did you live with?'

'My father.'

'Did you see your mother very often?'

His eyes met hers across the table and she was more than a little shocked at the hardness in his tone when he spoke.

'I never saw her alive again.'

Her eyes widened. 'Never?'

'She ran off with another man, a workmate of my father's.'

'That's terrible.' She bit her lip once more. 'You must have missed her so much.'

'I was soon taught not to miss her.'

She knew there was a wealth of information in that simple statement but wondered if it was wise to press him for too much more.

'I'm so sorry,' she said instead.

'Don't be.' He lifted his glass and drained it. He put it back down with a definitive clink on the table top and smiled. 'Now, what about hobbies?'

'Hobbies?'

'Things you like to do in your spare time.'

'I haven't had a lot of spare time just lately.'

'What if you had lots of free time and money was no object, what then?'

She tilted her head as she thought about it for a moment.

'I'd like to learn how to play the guitar.'

'Is that all?'

'And the cello and the piano and the flute and trumpet and—'

He laughed and held up a hand to stem her flow.

'What about your hobbies?' she asked.

'Like you, I don't have a lot of spare time but when I do I like to head into the bush where telephones can't reach me. I like to wake up to the sounds of birds, not traffic, and I don't want to hear the hum of electricity or computer terminals. I like the silence. In fact, I crave the silence.'

'Do you chop your own wood?'

'Sure do.'

'Do you ever take people with you?'

He gave her a long, intent look. 'No, not usually.'

'No girlfriend...or mistress?'

He shook his head. 'Most of the women I know would never understand my need for that kind of peace.'

She wasn't sure what to make of his answer. Was he telling her indirectly that she was the only woman he'd ever taken to his version of paradise?

'I expect most women would find it a bit daunting without modern conveniences.' She ran her finger over the rim of her glass once more.

'What about you?' he asked. 'How do you think you'd manage?'

'Well.' She lifted her gaze to his with a tremulous smile. 'I would need to be assured there were no spiders, but if I had access to a torch or candle I think I'd cope.'

'Are you frightened of the dark?'

It wasn't the first time he'd asked but she didn't see any point in avoiding the truth now.

'I am, actually.' She looked away, her colour high. 'I can't seem to help it. Ever since my mother died I found the dark intimidating. I hate admitting it but I've been sleeping with the light on since I was ten.'

'You should have told me.'

'How could I?' she asked. 'I don't know you, remember?'

'Forget about the game.' He frowned as he reached for her hand across the table. 'You should have told me about your phobia and about your inexperience.'

'Game or no game, I hardly knew you,' she pointed out. 'You forced me to marry you. A week to ten days is not a good time frame in which to feel comfortable enough to share one's innermost vulnerabilities.'

'Why did you marry me, Maddison?'

'Aren't we playing the I-don't-know-you game any more?'

'Not at the moment. Now answer my question.'

'You know why I married you,' she said. 'I did it to protect Kyle.'

'No other reason?'

She found it hard to hold his look. 'What other reason could there be?'

He leant back in his chair, his unwavering gaze unsettling her beyond endurance.

'I can think of one or two, but you mentioned once that you'd make me regret marrying you. How did you intend to bring that about?'

'I don't know.' She fluttered her free hand agitatedly. 'It was just a stupid emotion-driven threat. I wouldn't have the first idea of how to make you regret your actions. You seem to always get the upper hand no matter what I do or say.'

'You are getting to know me then,' he observed dryly.

She removed her hand from his and nursed it in her lap.

'I thought we were having a truce?' she said with a touch of resentment.

'We are.'

'You seem angry.'

'I can assure you I'm not.'

The waiter came to take their order and Maddison felt as if

Demetrius had timed his reappearance just so he could have the last word.

By the time their meals arrived the conversation had drifted to less dangerous topics, much to Maddison's relief. She didn't know what to make of him in this mood. On the one hand he seemed to want to lay down all ammunition but a small part of her remained wary of his motives.

'Would you like to go dancing somewhere?' he asked after they had eaten.

'I'm not much of a dancer.' She lowered her gaze somewhat shyly.

'I can teach you.'

'I'll step on your toes.'

'I have strong toes.'

'You'll need them,' she said as they got to their feet. 'I have high heels.'

He glanced down at them and his quick grimace was followed by a smile. 'We'll just have to take it one step at a time then, won't we?'

She gave him an answering smile but she couldn't help wondering if he was talking about their relationship and not dancing after all.

The nightclub he took her to was crowded but the music was good and Maddison couldn't help feeling the limited space made her lack of dancing skill largely irrelevant. She was so closely pressed against Demetrius's body she could feel every ridge of his abdomen along hers.

He turned her on the dance floor by slipping one steely muscled thigh between hers, sending a wave of sensation to the heating core of her body. She could feel the tug of desire deep within her and wondered if he could sense it. His eyes smouldered into hers as he moved with her about the floor, his arms around her waist, hers about his neck, each of their thighs moving as one.

It was hard to concentrate on the rhythm of the music with him so close. She could feel his warm breath caress her face as he looked down at her, a silent communication in his dark gaze.

Afterwards she couldn't precisely remember how they made it back to the car.

She recalled him whispering to her as the song ended, 'Let's get out of here,' and could still feel the way her spine had loosened at the sound of urgency in his tone.

She followed him out on legs not quite steady, her hand in his, her eyes glazed with a desire that threatened to overwhelm her in its intensity.

He drove the car with a ruthless precision that sent shivers of anticipation right through her. Each determined gear thrust she felt between her thighs as he weaved the powerful vehicle between the clotting traffic, the savage throaty roar of the engine sounding almost primal.

A few minutes later he swung the car into the hotel driveway and the valet parking attendant stepped forward for the keys.

Demetrius opened Maddison's door and she stepped out with her hand in the firm hold of his.

'Ready, darling?' His eyes burned into hers.

'And waiting,' she breathed.

The lift soared upwards as if it sensed the need for speed its occupants were silently communicating to each other as they stood shoulder to shoulder, staring at the illuminated lights above their heads.

Demetrius unlocked the penthouse door and she stepped through, turning to face him as he pushed the door closed with a flick of his hand.

He didn't speak.

He reached for his tie and wrenched it from his neck in such an intoxicatingly male fashion she felt her stomach give an instant somersault.

He only paused to undo a couple of buttons before hauling the shirt over his head and reaching for the buckle of his belt.

Maddison reached for the clip in her hair, shaking out the tresses with a toss of her head as she dropped the clip at his feet.

He stepped over it and, grasping her upper arms in his, pulled her in to him, his mouth coming down and covering hers in a kiss that seared her.

She felt his hands on the back fastener of her dress and heard the soft rustle of fabric as it slithered down her body to the floor as if in a sigh of surrender.

She stepped out of its pink circle, kicking off her shoes as she went.

He lifted his mouth from hers, his eyes drinking in her slim form, dressed in lacy push-up bra and g-string.

She pressed the palms of her hands against his chest and slithered down his body to tongue the cave of his navel, relishing in his sudden indrawn breath as she took the kiss lower and lower.

She undid his waistband and then slowly released his zip, peeling his trousers away with a determination that made him shiver in reaction.

'Maddison.' His voice came out as a harsh groan as her mouth moved towards him.

She tasted the steely length of him, delighting in the power of her mouth as he shuddered against its ministrations. She brought him to the brink, his hands buried in her hair, his breathing ragged, his legs braced as he fought for control.

He took her head in his hands and eased her from him, pushing her to the floor with a rough urgency that secretly thrilled her.

He wanted her and he wanted her now.

She felt it in every hard ridge of his body, she felt it in his lips and tongue, and she felt it as he pressed her backwards to receive his hardened length, shifting the tiny barrier of lace aside.

She gasped at the impact of his body within hers, the swollen heat of him stretching her until she felt him fill her completely.

She anchored herself by clasping his shoulders, her nails digging in as he drove on relentlessly with a barely controlled passion.

Her unbridled response to him seemed to only intensify his

fervid need, his breathing rate increasing with every movement of his body within hers.

She felt herself tip over the edge, the tumultuous waves carrying her off into oblivion where the mind and thought no longer existed.

She felt him tense and then the power of his release as he emptied himself, the silent shudders of intense pleasure secretly thrilling her.

She had brought him to this.

Demetrius took his time removing himself.

He loved the feel of her body around him, the way she held on to him as if she never wanted to let him go. It made him feel as if she might care for him in some as yet unconscious way.

He wanted her to care for him.

Damn it! He wanted her to love him.

Maddison reached for the pool of her dress as Demetrius got to his feet, her eyes avoiding his. She heard the slide of his zip and then the sound of him putting his shirt on.

'Maddison.'

She clutched the dress to her chest like a shield.

'I need to use the bathroom,' she said.

'I need to talk to you.'

'Can it wait?' She wrapped her dress around her like a sarong.

He clenched his hands to stop himself from tearing it off her.

'No, I'd like to discuss something important with you.'

She gave him a guarded look which annoyed him immensely. 'Well?'

He sent a hand through the wild disorder of his hair in a bid to stall for time. He wasn't sure of her mood. She'd been so responsive but now her guard was up and he didn't know if she was angry with him or herself.

'There's an important issue we need to discuss in the light of our sexual relationship.'

He saw her tense.

'You haven't got…anything…have you?' she asked.

'No, damn it! I haven't got anything but I am fertile.'

'Fertile?'

'I'm not shooting blanks.'

Maddison stared at him for a speechless moment as the reality of his words sank in.

'And, as far as I can tell, you're not on the pill, nor using any other type of contraceptive,' he continued.

'I'm not pregnant.'

'How can you be sure?'

'Surely I'd know if my own body got pregnant?' she threw at him. 'I'm not completely stupid. I'm expecting my period any day now.'

'I'm very glad to hear it.'

'I just bet you are.'

'What's that supposed to mean?'

She gave him a haughty look. 'Don't worry, Demetrius. I won't slap a paternity suit on you.'

'I wouldn't mind if you did.'

Her mouth fell open in shock. 'What do you mean?'

He bent to pick up his discarded tie, threading it through his fingers idly. 'I'm thirty-four years old. I'd not like to be too much older before I father a child or two.'

'A child or two?'

'A family.'

'You're surely not expecting me to…to…' She flapped her hands in panic and her dress slipped to the floor.

'Why not?' he asked. 'You're my wife, aren't you?'

'I'm a pretend wife!'

'So that little routine down here—' he pointed to where they had just made passionate love '—was nothing more than make-believe?'

'It was a moment of madness, that's what it was.' She snatched at her dress once more.

'You know what it was, so don't deny it.'

'What do you want me to say?' She turned on him. 'That I care something for you? After all you've done?'

He held her fiery look for as long as he could but he had to admit she'd made a very good point. How could he expect her to feel anything but the deepest loathing for him?

'I want you to think about it,' he said after a small pause.

'I've thought about it and no.'

'Is that your final word?'

'Of course it's my final word.'

'How soon will you know?'

'I know now. I told you—I'm not going to be your stupid breeding machine so—'

'I meant about your period.'

'I...' She did a rough calculation in her head. 'Today or tomorrow, maybe the next day.'

'You don't seem very sure.'

'I'm not a clock, you know!' She glared at him. 'Anyway, I'm often late.'

'You'll tell me as soon as you know?'

'It's none of your business.'

'I beg to differ but it is now very much my business. You could already be carrying my child.'

A funny sensation trickled into her belly at the thought of her body stretching to accommodate his baby, her abdomen taut, her breasts swollen, the unmistakable evidence of their passion growing inside her.

'I'm sure I won't be.'

'Just because you don't want something to happen doesn't ensure it won't.'

'I suppose you've done this deliberately?' she asked. 'Isn't this taking the pound of flesh a little too far?'

'I wasn't thinking when we made love.'

'We did not make love.' She sent him a frosty glance. 'We had sex.'

'Both produce babies.'

'I don't want to listen to this.' She turned away.

'There's something else I'd like to discuss with you.'

She stalled, a shiver of apprehension running through her at some indefinable element to his tone. 'What?'

'I don't want you to have any further contact with Jeremy Myalls.'

She opened and closed her mouth.

'May I ask why?' She finally found her voice.

'I don't trust him.'

'I see.'

He wanted to tell her of his suspicions regarding Jeremy's handling of the investigation into her father's misuse of company funds but wasn't sure she was in the right frame of mind to accept his angle on the matter.

'Is there anyone else I'm forbidden to have contact with?' she asked with her usual spirit.

'No.' He hooked his jacket over his shoulder and turned for the door.

'Where are you going?' she asked before she could stop herself.

He gave her an ironic look as he turned the doorknob.

'I'm going out. Any objections?'

She ground her teeth. 'No. I don't give a damn.'

'I'm very glad to hear it,' he said and closed the door behind him.

Maddison shut her eyes against the bitter tears but there was no stopping them. She stumbled blindly for the spare bedroom but it was very close to dawn before she finally fell asleep.

Maddison tried not to notice the fact that Demetrius hadn't returned to the penthouse overnight. She avoided looking at his smoothly made bed on the way past, and after a solitary breakfast made her way downstairs.

She went to the nearest auto teller machine and checked her balance, her eyes instantly widening at the amount documented there.

Jeremy had deposited the funds so all she had to do now was withdraw them.

She made her way inside the next branch of her bank that she came to but when she handed her withdrawal slip to the teller she gave her an apologetic look.

'I'm sorry, those funds can't be withdrawn until they clear.'

'How long will that take?'

The teller looked at her computer screen for a moment.

'Five working days for the Australian currency and a month for the international ones.'

'International?'

'International cheques take up to one month to clear. I'm sorry.'

Maddison left the bank in a state of agitation. She'd wanted to hand over a bank cheque to Demetrius, not have those funds sitting in her bank account for a month!

She had only moved a few paces back through the hotel foyer when a male voice called out to her.

'Maddison!'

'Kyle?'

She turned on her heel and threw herself at him, almost choking him with her arms around his neck.

'Hey, steady on, old girl.' He extricated himself with a gruff note of affection in his voice.

'What are you doing here?' she asked, her expression instantly clouding.

'I wanted to see you. Mr Marquis gave me an advance so I could come.'

'You can't see me here!'

'Why not?'

'You know why not!'

'Let's go upstairs then,' he suggested.

She bit her lip in indecision.

'Come on, Maddy, I won't keep you long.'

'All right,' she said, leading the way. 'But I'm warning you if the axe falls on your neck this time I'm not stepping on to the block with you.'

The lift carried them upstairs in a mutually agreed silence.

Maddison shut the penthouse door behind them and faced him.

'Kyle, you really shouldn't be here.'

'I know but I had to tell you something important.'

'What could be more important than you staying out of jail?'

'I didn't sink his boat.'

It took her a moment to grasp his simple statement.

'What?'

'I didn't do it.'

She stared at him in horror. 'What do you mean you didn't do it? You told me you did it! You said you sabotaged his boat…I mean his yacht, and it sank!'

'I admit I was on his yacht that night,' he said. 'And I wanted to sink it but I didn't do it. I couldn't have.'

'I'm not following you.' She lowered herself on to the nearest sofa.

He reached for a newspaper clipping in his pocket and handed it to her. 'I found this in one of the newspapers at Gillaroo. It says Demetrius's boat was sabotaged by a diving spear. I pulled the plug out of the centre of his yacht, thinking it would do the trick, but it wasn't enough to sink it.'

'You didn't use a diving spear?'

'Sis, I can't swim to save myself. How the hell do you think I'd be able to pull off that sort of stunt?'

'I thought someone must have helped you…' She swallowed and stared at the newspaper clipping in her hand. It showed a picture of Demetrius's yacht after its retrieval from the bottom of Parsley Bay, the underside of it clearly scored by three deep puncture marks.

She lifted her confused gaze to his. 'But if you didn't do it, then who did?'

CHAPTER THIRTEEN

'I DON'T know, but I have a feeling it won't be long before they reveal themselves,' Kyle answered confidently.

'What makes you say that?'

He gave her a superior male look. 'Because Demetrius has known almost from the start where I was.'

Her eyes widened in shock. *'What?'*

'He called me the other day.'

She got to her feet in agitation, her tumbled thoughts scrambling her brain.

'But I don't understand.' She gripped the back of the drinks cabinet for support. 'He kept asking me to tell him where you were.'

'Maybe he wanted you to trust him.'

'I don't know how to deal with this.' She sat down again. 'Why did he marry me if he didn't need to know where you were?'

'Maybe he fancies you.'

She knew her colour was giving her away but there was nothing she could do about it.

'Or maybe he felt guilty about what happened to Dad,' he added more solemnly. 'He hinted at it on the telephone. It seems he was preoccupied at the time of Dad's trouble with the unexpected death of his mother.'

'He told you that?'

'Yeah, he seemed pretty open about it actually. Said how losing a mother so young through divorce had made him run off the rails a bit.' He lowered his gaze to stare at his scuffed Blundstone boots. 'I could really relate to what he was saying.'

Maddison stared at her brother as if seeing someone entirely different.

'I'm sorry for all the trouble I've caused,' he added. 'I've been a right jerk, I know, but it's taken till now to see it. Demetrius really helped me to see how the past can have such an impact on your future unless you get some insight.' He straightened to his full gangling height, determination in his tone as he faced her. 'I'm going back to the Territory in a few hours. I've got a muster to do and once that's over I'm going back to school.'

'School?'

'Don't look so shocked.' He grinned. 'That's another thing your husband taught me in the space of a single phone call. You can't get anywhere in life without an education.'

Tears brightened her eyes as she hugged him.

'Be happy, Maddy,' he said gruffly.

'I'll try,' she promised.

Kyle had not long left for his return trip to the Northern Territory when Maddison heard Demetrius's key in the lock. He came into the lounge a few moments later, his brooding expression as his eyes met hers striking a chord of disquiet deep inside her.

'Hi.' She tried a smile but it didn't quite work.

He didn't answer but his eyes glinted darkly as he unclipped the metal fastener on his briefcase as he laid it down on the coffee table between them. He took out a sheet of paper and handed it to her.

'Want to tell me about this or am I supposed to guess?' His cold, terse tone sent a trickle of alarm through her.

She stared at the paper in her hands, her throat closing over when she saw it was a bank statement.

Her bank statement.

'I…I can explain…'

'I suggest you do so before you find yourself before a High Court judge.'

She blinked at him in shock. 'Surely you don't mean that?'

His eyes were almost black with anger. 'Do you think that

just because you slept with me I would overlook something like this? What sort of fool do you take me for?'

'I...I can explain—' The bank statement fluttered to the floor as she twisted her hands in front of her agitatedly. 'I was only doing it to protect—'

His cynical snort cut off her speech and sent another chill down her back. 'I suppose this is the payback you had planned all along?' His mouth twisted bitterly. 'You promised me you were going to make me regret marrying you, and damn you to hell, you did it.'

'But you don't understand!'

'Oh, I understand.' He came towards her, stopping just inches away from her trembling form, his eyes raking her mercilessly. 'I understand that you and Jeremy Myalls had planned this for months.'

She frowned in confusion. Had Jeremy told him that?

He slammed his fist against the wall beside her, making her shrink away in alarm. 'Do you know what gets me the most? I thought you were different. I thought I had finally found someone I could trust with my life.'

'Demetrius, I...' She gulped as his eyes flashed with hatred, the rest of her sentence frozen on her trembling mouth.

'But you didn't get away with it, Maddison.' The line of his mouth was rigid. 'I made sure of that. I've been watching Jeremy for weeks. I knew he was up to something. What I didn't know was how willing a partner in crime you would turn out to be.'

'I didn't do—'

'Are you going to stand there and lie?' He almost shouted the words. 'Damn it, Maddison, I have proof. That is your bank statement, isn't it?'

Her gaze flicked to the damning paper on the floor beneath their feet. 'Yes.'

'And, correct me if I'm wrong, but the funds in there are mine on behalf of foreign investors, are they not?'

'Yes.' She swallowed again. 'I was going to get them out to give to you but the bank wouldn't release them. I didn't know that there was international money involved and it takes a month for it to clear. I was hoping to withdraw them immediately and—'

'You expect me to believe that?'

She stood before him uncertainly. 'I know it looks bad but...'

'Why should I believe you?'

It was a good question, she had to grant him that.

'Demetrius, surely you don't think I would do something like that. I was trying to help you—'

He tilted her chin so that she had to meet the burning fury in his gaze. 'You wanted my pride and you nearly got it, God damn you.' He dropped his hand and stepped back from her. 'I want you out of here by the time I get back.'

'What?' Her stomach caved in at his curt dismissal.

'You heard.'

'Demetrius, I—'

'I'm giving you the chance to get away before I press charges,' he said, cutting her off again. 'Jeremy hasn't been quite so lucky.'

He turned and left the penthouse without another word, the door snapping shut behind him with an ominous stroke of finality.

Maddison fought back tears but it was no good. The choking sobs tore at her chest as she sank to the floor where, through her tears, she saw the bank statement with her name printed clearly on the top.

She left the penthouse a short time later, her head down as she went past reception in case any of the staff noticed her reddened eyes and still wobbling chin.

She slipped into the first cab that came along and when the driver asked for her destination she felt another wave of distress hit her. She choked back a sob and reached for the store of tissues up her sleeve, trying to avoid the driver's concerned gaze in the rear vision mirror.

'Where to, lady?' the driver asked after they'd gone around the block.

She lifted her face out of the wad of sodden tissues and met his eyes in the mirror. 'Do you know where Black Rock Mountain is?'

The driver frowned. 'Never heard of it. Is it very far from the city?'

'Not far enough,' she said wryly and, giving him some directions, sat back in her seat and pulled out yet another tissue.

Demetrius came back to the penthouse late that night, fully expecting Maddison to still be there in direct defiance of his orders. He knew she wouldn't be able to resist the opportunity to gloat over her final victory, bringing about the revenge she had promised.

How well she had achieved it!

He slammed the door to announce his arrival, sure it would drive her out for yet another confrontation.

Silence.

He frowned as he searched through the apartment, his throat tightening when he realised she wasn't there.

He turned and saw something lying on the floor next to the bank statement he'd waved under her nose. He bent down to pick it up, his fingers closing around it just like the invisible tension squeezing around his heart.

It was a very wet tissue...

Maddison paid the cab driver with all the money she had in her purse once they arrived at the hut at Black Rock Mountain.

'You sure you'll be all right?' he asked as he gave the remote hideaway a quick, almost nervous, glance. 'There doesn't seem to be too much out here.'

'There's not, but I prefer it that way.' She closed the car door and waved him off, fighting off panic as the darkness of night settled around her like a smothering cloak once the car lights had faded into the distance.

She pushed open the door of the hut and, trying to ignore the fear tiptoeing up her spine, reached for the matches on the mantelpiece.

She struck one and breathed a sigh of relief when the soft glow illuminated the heavy darkness. There were still some pieces of tinder amongst the wood in the basket by the fireplace so she made a rough pile with them and, striking a fresh match, watched as the flames took hold, casting a welcome flickering light to the far reaches of the room.

Once the fire was burning steadily she curled up in front of it with a blanket off the bed and, burying her face in its soft folds, tried not to notice how it still held a trace of Demetrius's aftershave.

She closed her eyes and listened to the sounds of the night outside—the soft chirrup of crickets, the throaty call of a tree frog looking for a mate and the sound of water trickling through the bed of the creek...

Demetrius threatened to sack the entire staff of the hotel for not being able to tell him where Maddison had gone.

'She got into a taxi,' one of the junior porters said, under threat of instant dismissal.

'Which one?' Demetrius eyeballed him.

The porter pointed to one of the cabs outside. 'That was the company; why don't you ask them to do a trace?'

Demetrius turned on his heel and after a few terse words with the driver came back inside. 'I want my car and I want it immediately.'

The junior porter gave him a nervous look. 'Which one, sir?'

'The four-wheel drive, and if it's not here in under thirty seconds you're fired.'

'Yes, sir.'

A short time later Demetrius was on his way, his hands around the wheel white-knuckled in tension.

He'd thought he had it all worked out, the way Jeremy had conspired with Maddison to bring about the revenge they both sought, but if that was so why had she left his apartment in tears? Had he misjudged her? What if Jeremy was lying? After all, what was one more lie, considering all the others he'd managed to pull off over the years?

He frowned as he drove through the encroaching darkness. How had he got it so wrong? She'd only married him to protect her younger wilful brother. Her threats had been little more than an attempt at salvaging her pride at the way he'd railroaded her into an arrangement that was nothing if not distasteful to her.

His gut clenched at the way he'd broken their agreement. If anyone should be accused of lying it should be him. He'd wanted her from the first day he'd called at her flat, her flashing blue eyes defying him to do his worst. Her innocence had been a total shock to him, and now that he'd had time to think about it, it explained a lot about her that he'd previously overlooked. She wasn't some grasping opportunist after a fast buck. She was a devoted sister who had been prepared to sacrifice herself so her brother could escape punishment.

The hut was in darkness when he arrived and for a heart-stopping moment he wondered if the information he'd been given had been wrong. But on opening the door he shone his torch around and saw her curled up in front of the now dead fire, her hair across her cheek, her small hand like a starfish where it rested on the blanket.

He sat on the rickety chair and watched her sleep until the sun came over the horizon and shone its warming rays of light through the window.

Maddison opened her eyes to find Demetrius sitting watching her and from what she could tell of his darkly shadowed eyes he'd been doing so for quite a while.

She brushed her hair out of her face as she struggled upright, her eyes skilfully avoiding his.

'Why did you come here, Maddison?' he asked, his voice containing no trace of the anger of the evening before.

'I'm sorry…' She got to her feet and headed for the door. 'I'll leave straight away.'

'To go where?'

She gave him a nervous glance over her shoulder. 'I'm not sure…I'll find somewhere.'

'On foot?'

She bit her lip. 'If I have to.'

'Is my company so distasteful to you?'

She lowered her gaze. 'No.'

'Why didn't you tell me you had nothing to do with Jeremy's plot to siphon off money from my company?'

'I tried to tell you but you wouldn't listen.'

'I mean right from the start,' he said. 'Why didn't you come to me as soon as you knew what he was up to? You had no need to compromise yourself in such a way.'

Her eyes came back to his. 'I didn't know if you would believe me. You hadn't believed my father; why would you listen to me?'

His expression clouded with guilt. 'I made a big mistake with my handling of your father's situation. I can't change that. I was distracted by the death of my mother and relied too heavily on Jeremy to sort things out.' He scraped a hand through his hair and continued. 'I have since learnt the details of the arrangement Jeremy made with your father over the loan. All I can say is that I'm sorry I didn't see his ruthless behaviour before now; fewer people would have been hurt if I had.'

She gave him a direct look. 'How long have you known where Kyle was?'

'I knew where Kyle was within days of him leaving for the Northern Territory.'

'Why did you pretend you didn't know? You could have sent him to prison at any time and I wouldn't have been able to stop you.'

'I would've, except I realised he didn't sink my yacht.'

She stared at him for a long moment. 'How did you know?'

'You said that Kyle couldn't swim very well and I came to the conclusion he could never have done it, or at least not without considerable help.'

'Do you know who did it?'

'Surely you don't need me to tell you?'

'Jeremy?'

'Got it in one.'

Maddison gnawed her lip for a moment as her confused thoughts ran together in a blur. 'But I don't understand why you insisted on me marrying you if you already knew where Kyle was. I don't see the point. What did you hope to gain by it?'

His dark eyes meshed with hers, the corner of his mouth lifting in a wry smile. 'You can't guess?'

'You said it was a smokescreen. I know Elena Tsoulis is your mistress.'

'I haven't seen Elena since the day of our marriage.'

'You haven't?' Hope sprang in her chest as she looked up at him.

He shook his head. 'I had much more important things on my mind. Like trying to get you to fall in love with me so our marriage could be permanent instead of temporary.'

She blinked at him. 'But…but I thought you had no intention of being tied down. You warned me not to get attached to you. You made it clear you didn't trust long-term promises.'

'I've learnt a lot about myself over the last few days,' he confessed. 'A lot of it I haven't liked. I'd always insisted my mother's desertion hadn't affected me but my pattern of relationships up until now has proved that isn't the case. I never stayed with any lover long enough for my feelings to become engaged, that is until I met you. Within a few days of meeting you I realised I had met the one woman who could unlock my heart. I fell in love with everything about you—your undivided loyalty to your brother and your unerring defiance even when you were scared. It was a pretty heady mixture, wrapped up in a small but totally desirable body which seemed unable to resist my touch.'

Maddison stared at him, not sure she was hearing him correctly.

'When I met you that day at your flat it occurred to me I had never met anyone who would go so far out on a limb for someone else. Initially I thought I'd test you, to see how far you'd actually go, but within a very short time I realised I was the one prepared to do anything to keep you, even blackmail.'

'Why did you ask me to leave last night?'

He grimaced as if the memory of what he'd said still pained him. 'I was blindingly angry. I didn't stop to think if I'd misjudged the situation. When Jeremy told me you and he had been in cahoots, plotting revenge, I saw every tone of red. It was only later when I came back to the penthouse and found your damp tissue on the floor that I realised I may have misinterpreted something. I couldn't understand why you'd be crying if everything Jeremy had said was true.' He came and stood nearer, his hand going to her chin to lift up her face to meet his eyes. 'Why were you crying?'

'I didn't want to leave you...'

'Why not?' His voice was deep and husky, his eyes dark and smouldering as they held hers.

'I know you told me not to, but I just couldn't help it. I fell in love with you.'

'Even though I blackmailed you into marriage?'

'I think especially because of that. I was so busy fighting you I didn't realise what was happening until it was too late.'

'Don't remind me of how ruthless I was,' he said. 'I still cringe to think of how I rushed you into bed.'

'You regret it?' Her expression clouded.

'I don't regret it one bit.' He took her hands in his. 'I do, however, feel as if I railroaded you into a relationship you weren't quite ready for.'

She looped her arms around his neck, pressing herself closer.

'What makes you think I'm not ready?'

He smiled down into her sparkling blue eyes, his heart swelling with love.

'I think I'm going to need a little more convincing,' he said. 'Call me suspicious, but I like to be absolutely certain before I make long-term commitments.'

'What would convince you?'

'I don't know.' He drew her even closer. 'Any suggestions?'

'How about this?' She pressed a soft kiss to his mouth.

'Not bad,' he said after a few minutes. 'But I think it's going to take a bit more to bring me round completely.'

Maddison's fingers went to the knot of his tie, loosening it and drawing it through the collar of his shirt to let it fall to the floor at their feet.

'How about this?' She trailed a hot blaze of feathery kisses down his neck, opening his shirt button by button to continue on over the flat plane of his abdomen.

'Convinced yet?' She looked up at him briefly as her fingers went to the buckle of his leather belt.

'Not entirely.' He sucked in a breath as the belt slid to the floor to join his tie.

'Am I getting close?'

'Very close,' he answered and, hauling her upright, scooped her in his arms and carried her towards the bedroom.

'Shouldn't you be at work instead of being out here in the wilderness?' she asked as he shouldered open the door.

His dark chocolate gaze glittered with naked desire as he looked down at her smiling face.

'I've got better things to do right now.'

'I thought that to billionaires making money was the most important thing.'

'There is one thing much more important to this particular billionaire than making money,' he said.

'Oh?' She wriggled out of her tracksuit and dimpled up at him. 'What is that?'

He pressed an open mouthed kiss to the creamy upper curve of her breast, lingering over the taut nipple before travelling to the soft under-swell.

She sucked in a tight little breath. 'Aren't...you going to tell me?'

'No.' He grinned down at her wolfishly. 'I'm going to show you instead.'

4 FREE

BOOKS AND A SURPRISE GIFT!

We would like to take this opportunity to thank you for reading this Mills & Boon® book by offering you the chance to take FOUR more specially selected titles from the Modern Romance™ series absolutely FREE! We're also making this offer to introduce you to the benefits of the Reader Service™—

- ★ FREE home delivery
- ★ FREE gifts and competitions
- ★ FREE monthly Newsletter
- ★ Exclusive Reader Service offers
- ★ Books available before they're in the shops

Accepting these FREE books and gift places you under no obligation to buy, you may cancel at any time, even after receiving your free shipment. Simply complete your details below and return the entire page to the address below. You don't even need a stamp!

YES! Please send me 4 free Modern Romance books and a surprise gift. I understand that unless you hear from me, I will receive 6 superb new titles every month for just £2.75 each, postage and packing free. I am under no obligation to purchase any books and may cancel my subscription at any time. The free books and gift will be mine to keep in any case.

P5ZED

Ms/Mrs/Miss/Mr ....Initials ....
BLOCK CAPITALS PLEASE

Surname ....

Address ....

....

....Postcode..................................

Send this whole page to:
UK: FREEPOST CN81, Croydon, CR9 3WZ